The Sea Witch

Anni Stewart

AuthorHouse™ UK Ltd.
1663 Liberty Drive
Bloomington, IN 47403 USA
www.authorhouse.co.uk
Phone: 0800.197.4150

Published by AuthorHouse 09/23/2013

ISBN: 978-1-4918-7905-4 (sc)
ISBN: 978-1-4918-7906-1 (e)

For Jessica and Victoria,
with a big thank you to Mairead for her wisdom
and support

Chapter 1

The bedroom looked as if it had been hit by a hurricane. Drawers were hanging open, and there were items of clothing scattered over the beds and furniture, whilst in the middle of the room, Lucy struggled to close the zip of an overstuffed suitcase. Suddenly, she lost her grip and tumbled backwards onto the floor, where she was immediately joined by her twin sister, Ellie, who had rolled off the top of the case, where she had been trying to use her weight to squash it closed from above. They had stood on it, sat on it, and stood and sat on it at the same time, and now they both sat on the bedroom floor giggling, their faces red from the effort—and the case still unzipped.

"I've another idea," said Lucy as she tried to control her laughter. "One of us can stand on the case and carefully walk around to squeeze the edges together, whilst the other one pulls the zip." She pouted her lips and blew out a huge sigh.

Ellie pretended to look puzzled, and then, after a few seconds, said, "Right. I think I understand what you're saying. Let's give it a go. You're much heavier than me," she teased, "so you can be the one who goes on top this time."

"I don't think so," replied Lucy with a grin. "Your bum looked much bigger than mine when you were crawling on top of the case just now." They both shrieked as they aimed friendly slaps at each other, knowing that as identical twins they were just about the same height and shape. In fact, when each looked in a mirror, she saw an image of the other twin: a girl with a pretty, oval face framed by shiny, shoulder-length black hair, a few freckles scattered across rosy cheeks, and eyes the colour of milk chocolate. They continued to giggle, only stopping and looking at each other wide eyed and open mouthed when their mother called from downstairs.

"Are you two girls nearly ready with your case? Dad's already loaded ours into the car, so please get a move on."

The twins shrugged their shoulders and continued with the task before them. Lucy stood on the case, and Ellie prepared to pull the zip. Much to their amazement, the zip eventually reached the end of the opening, and the job was done. They high-fived each other and then collapsed onto the floor, exhausted by the effort that they had put into closing the case but happy that they wouldn't have to take any more of their clothes out to start again. Now they just had to pack a small bag each with any personal items that they might need for their three-week stay at their grandparents' home by the sea, in Devon.

Every year, during their school's summer break, Ellie and Lucy went to Devon with their parents, Peter and Sally Bennett, but this year Peter and Sally were going to Switzerland. They were both doctors involved in research and had been invited to take part in a multinational medical conference. The conference was just for one week, but they had decided that, as they had never been to that part of Europe, they would spend some time holidaying before re-joining their daughters for a night or two before they all returned home.

Ellie and Lucy loved the area where their grandparents lived, so they were not too disappointed to be spending time there without their mum and dad. They adored Gran and Gramps, as they affectionately called them, and looked forward to being spoiled by them. They were also looking forward to spending lots of time on the beach, where they enjoyed searching the rock pools for unusual shells and sea creatures, as well as swimming in the beautiful green-blue water. They also liked playing beach cricket with Gramps and any other visitors to the beach who wished to join in. Best of all, though, they loved taking the ferry across the estuary; it was the quickest and easiest way to reach the small town opposite. The only other access was by car, but as this was a fairly long drive, people tended to rely upon the ferry. In the summer months, two or three ferries were often needed to cope with the high number of people wishing to cross over from the town to one of several golden, sandy bays. It was on one of these that Ellie and Lucy loved to spend their days. Their grandparents' home, which was situated at the top of the cliffs, was named Beaches because of the number of small sandy bays that could be seen from the back of the house. At the end of the garden, where the ground dropped to the beach, there was iron fencing, with a gate opening onto a flight of stone steps and strong handrails leading down to the rocks and sand below.

Just as the girls had closed their case and collapsed on the floor, panting and laughing, their mother poked her head around the bedroom door.

"Ten more minutes, girls, and then Dad wants to pack your luggage into the car. He's aiming to set off in half an hour so that we arrive at Gran and Gramps's house by lunchtime. Dad and I can then have something to eat and drink with you all before setting off for the airport, and you two girls will have the whole afternoon to spend on the beach. How does that sound?"

"Sounds good, Mum," the girls chorused. "We're almost ready."

"Great! I'll go and tell Dad. Are you both sure you've packed everything you'll need? Don't forget that you will be away for three weeks."

"Mum, stop worrying," said Ellie. "We've packed so much, Dad will have a job carrying the case downstairs for us, and Gran won't need to do too much washing, as we'll have plenty of changes of clothing."

"Yep," chipped in Lucy, "and anyway, we'll make sure that we bring all of our dirty stuff home for you to wash, Mum, as we know how much you love washing."

Their mother laughed at this, knowing perfectly well that the girls' Gran would make sure that they returned with all their clothes washed and ironed. She then tried to pick up the case, pretending to struggle with it. "Goodness, it feels like you've packed sufficient to last half a dozen holidays, let alone one. I'll go and tell Dad that we are almost ready and just hope that he doesn't hurt his back carrying the case. Oh, and before we go, please tidy your hair. You both look like you've been dragged through a hedge backwards."

When their mother had gone back downstairs, they set about packing their individual bags. They both loved to draw, so in went pads and pencils, along with the books they wanted to read. Ellie had her favourite big old teddy with its ears chewed off and Lucy her pink floppy-eared rabbit equally as chewed, toys they had since they were toddlers. Now twelve years old, they still enjoyed having them to cuddle in bed at night. A number of other important items, including their laptop, went into the bags before they pulled their hair back off their faces and secured the bunches with scrunchies, a plain blue one for Ellie to match her blue striped T-shirt and jeans, and for Lucy a sparkly pink one to go with her pink blouse, pink cotton cut-offs and pink trainers. They then declared themselves ready for the journey.

Fifteen minutes later, the car was packed, the house checked and checked again to make sure that all electrical items were unplugged, windows closed, and taps turned off. Lastly, spare keys were given to Bill and Jenny, the next-door neighbours, who were going to look after the house whilst the family was away.

Everyone finally took their seat in the car, and with Dad driving, they began their journey to Devon from their home in Somerset. It was still only 9.30 a.m.

When the family arrived at Gran and Gramps's house, they were met with hugs and kisses as well as cold drinks, sandwiches, and Gran's homemade cakes. After lunch was finished and goodbyes had been said, Peter and Sally left to begin their journey to Switzerland. They promised to text the girls the next day.

After their parents had left, the twins asked their grandparents if they could go down to the beach. They knew the rules about not going near the water without an adult being present but didn't mind being reminded once again. Gramps had told them that the tide had recently turned and was on its way out, and they knew that this would leave the rock pools full of sea water and interesting sea life. Putting on their rubber beach shoes, the two girls started down to the beach. They spent some time exploring the rock pools and the beach, whilst at the same time chatting and making plans for what they were going to do the next day.

As always, time passed quickly when the twins were absorbed in checking out the contents of the pools, so that when Ellie looked at her watch, she wasn't at all surprised to see that it was almost five o'clock. Turning to her sister, who was lost in her own rock-pool world, she asked, "Hey, sis, do you know what time it is?"

Lucy jumped, startled by Ellie's intrusion into her thoughts. She looked up at her sister, flicked her long dark hair back from where it had fallen across her face, and said, "No. I haven't a clue."

"Nearly five o'clock," replied Ellie. "What do you think? Had we better go up to the house?"

"S'pose so, though it's a shame, as this pool is full of these tiny crabs that keep burrowing in and out of the sand, and it's fascinating to watch them." She held her hand out to show her sister a crab that was running about on her palm. "I'd love to stay longer, but I guess we might as well go up now and sort out our things; then Gran won't grumble at us. You know how she likes things done right away, just like Mum."

Ellie nodded in agreement and pulled a long face. "It's magic here on the beach. It really would be great to stay, but I guess if we do the unpacking now it gets it over and done with, and I agree with you it will keep Gran happy. Let's just have five more minutes and then go up. Anyway, it will be great to see our room again. I hope we still have the one overlooking the beach. I love waking up in the mornings and watching the sea from the window. This is going to be a fab holiday! I just have this great feeling about it."

"Me too," said Lucy.

The twins returned to searching the rock pools for a few more minutes before heading towards the steps that led up to Beaches. Their grandmother had seen them approaching through the kitchen window, and wiping her floury hands on her apron, she greeted them with a big smile, saying, "In you come, girls. Did you enjoy the beach? Nothing ever really changes down there; it's just as you left it when you were last here." She put her arms around the twins. "It's so lovely to have you here again. We are going to have such a good time together."

"It's always great to be here with you and Gramps," said Ellie. "And the beach is just as wonderful as it always is, but we thought that we had better leave it for today and unpack." Lucy nodded in agreement with what her sister was saying.

Gran was impressed, thinking to herself how much the girls had matured since their last visit. At one time they would have protested at the idea of leaving the beach to unpack their cases. Now they were actually keen to get it done. How times had changed!

"Right," said Gran. "You're in the same room, and everything is ready for you. Gramps has carried your bags upstairs. Good job he is strong, as that big case is quite heavy." The twins smiled knowingly.

"Yes, Dad said it was the heaviest case he'd ever lifted," said Ellie. "We thought that he was going to make us take out some of the things we'd packed, but he didn't, thank goodness. It took me and Lucy ages to get the zip closed, and we didn't fancy doing it again. Luckily we were running out of time, and Dad just put it in the boot."

Gran smiled as the girls raced for the stairs and up to the bedroom they were to share for the next three weeks. It was a large attic room painted sunshine yellow. They stood at the huge window that overlooked the water and gave them a wonderful view across to the other side of the estuary, where they could see two large yachts moored. There were also a number of smaller boats sailing up and down the estuary, as well as passenger ferries going back and forth, full of holidaymakers and local people. The skyline above the shimmering water was clustered with houses, hotels, and other buildings that had been there for many years.

When all of their belongings had been unpacked, the bedroom no longer looked like a spare room. Dressing gowns and colourful PJs lay on the bed, anoraks hung on the hook behind the door, while the drawers and cupboards were stuffed to bursting. The two girls glowed with satisfaction before putting the finishing touches to the room. Big Ted was laid on Ellie's bed, and Sammy Rabbit sat on Lucy's. Their suitcase, which would not be needed for another three weeks, had been pushed under one of the beds. Satisfied with their work and ready for their evening meal, they quickly cleaned themselves up and went back downstairs to join their grandparents.

"Just in time, as I'm about to serve up," called out Gran from the kitchen.

After a delicious meal of chicken, crispy roast potatoes and beans from Gran and Gramps own vegetable garden, Lucy and Ellie helped with the washing up. As they felt quite tired after their busy day, they turned down Gramps's offer of a walk. He smiled and gave them each a hug, at the same time saying to Gran, "As the girls aren't coming with me, and seeing as it's a fine evening, I'll go for a long one, so don't worry if I'm not back for a couple of hours or so." Ellie nudged Lucy, giving her a look that said they had made the right decision. Having spent previous holidays with their grandparents, they knew how far and how fast their grandfather could walk. When Gramps had left, the two girls settled in large squidgy armchairs in the comfortable living room, each with her favourite book, but it wasn't too long before their eyes were closing and their heads nodding. Seeing this, Gran suggested that they have an early night. They were too tired to protest and were soon fast asleep in comfortable beds, covered in soft duvets.

Chapter 2

The following morning, the twins were up and about early, dressed for the beach. As the sun was shining, they had on shorts and sun tops—everything pink for Lucy, right down to her rubber shoes, and blue for Ellie, with the exception of a large yellow sunflower that was printed on the front of her T-shirt.

On previous visits they had been allowed to have a large glass bowl in their room, which they had filled with seawater so that they could safely keep any interesting shells or sea creatures that they might find on the beach or in rock pools. They always put some sand, small rocks, and plant life in the bowl, to ensure that the living creatures had as natural a habitat as possible and were not harmed in any way, and at the end of their holiday they would return their collection to the sea before going home. They had discussed whether or not to ask if they could have the bowl in their room once again but had decided that, as they were now twelve, it might be considered a bit childish. Maybe they would just have to do their drawings down on the beach. They loved making sketches of their more interesting finds, and each had several sketch pads full of lovely detailed drawings from previous holidays.

Whilst Gran was busy sorting out the breakfast in the kitchen, the twins talked with their grandfather about their plans for the day ahead. Suddenly Gramps reached under the table and, to their surprise, came up holding the glass fish bowl, all clean and shining.

"Thought you might want this in your room again, but as you haven't asked for it . . . well, I wondered if you had outgrown—"

"Oh no, we haven't," Ellie quickly interrupted, whilst Lucy just grinned. "We can't wait to go down onto the beach to fetch the water and sand to sort out the bowl before we start looking for things to put in it. Isn't that right, Lucy?"

Lucy, the quieter of the sisters, nodded and grinned yet again, happy to let her twin speak for her.

"Don't worry about carrying up too much water," said Gramps. "I'll do that for you. Those steps up to the house are quite steep, and knowing you two girls, you will have your buckets full up with what you've collected, and there'll be enough for you to carry."

"Thanks, Gramps," was the joint response.

Gran appeared from the kitchen a couple of minutes later with two plates of bacon and eggs. "This'll give you all the energy you will need for a morning on the beach," she said as she placed a plate in front of each of them. "Eat up while it's warm. Gramps and I have had ours already." The girls did not need to be told twice.

As Ellie and Lucy tucked into their food, Gramps lowered the morning paper that he had been reading, saying to his wife, "There's an article here about the increase in smuggling along this part of the coastline. Apparently, yachts are regularly being used to smuggle illegal drugs, as well as people, into the country."

The twins, who had finished eating, were listening with interest to what Gramps was saying.

"Do you think that they would use our beaches?" asked Lucy, feeling both excited and worried at the same time.

"I don't think so," Gramps quickly responded, worried that maybe he shouldn't have spoken about this in front of his granddaughters. Wishing to reassure them, he said, "I should think that they would need places to drop anchor and unload onto smaller vessels, and our small bays probably wouldn't be suitable or private enough." Pointing to the paper, he added, "Anyway, it also says here that Customs officers have been provided with fast boats to stop and search the yachts at sea, so most of them probably don't get as far as land on this part of the coastline. Now, Cornwall is another matter, as there are lots of isolated landing places, and that's where smugglers a long time ago used to bring in alcohol, especially brandy, to avoid paying taxes.

Lucy made a mental note to look this up when she was next using her laptop.

After breakfast, Gran gave the two girls a reminder of the beach rules, which included the need for them to stay together and to return to the house by 1 p.m. for lunch. She also cautioned them to be careful when climbing to get to the rock pools and reminded them once again that there was no swimming unless either she or Gramps was on the beach with them. Their toes were curling inside their shoes and their fingers twitching behind their backs as they listened politely but wished that Gran would finish so they could go down to the beach. Finally Gran said, "I know that you're getting older and more responsible, but Gramps and I would worry so much if we were not there when you are swimming. We know that you are both very good swimmers and would probably be quite safe on your own, but nevertheless, we still want to be there. So humour us. You are so precious, we just want you to be safe." Then she drew them both into her arms for a group hug.

"Okay, Gran," agreed both girls.

"Away with you then, and enjoy yourself. I will see you at lunchtime. Oh, and I've left a carrier bag at the back door with some snacks and drinks for you to take down to the beach. Please don't forget to bring the empties back," she said with smile. Nodding in acknowledgement, Lucy and Ellie set off for the beach, loaded down with large plastic buckets, small nets, and the carrier bag filled with goodies.

The first thing they did was just stand at the water's edge and watch all the morning activities. They were always enthralled by the boats that came in various sizes, from the small dinghies to the old well-used fishing boats and large yachts, some of which were all shiny and new. However, their favourite sea vessel was the ferry, with its red, white, and blue bunting that flapped in the sea breeze. This ferry was different from those that carried passengers back and forth across the estuary. It was larger; it picked up passengers at the marina in the town before taking them to another beach further up the estuary. Then there were other large boats, which took passengers on hour-long trips around the many different creeks and golden beaches along the shoreline.

As it was still quite early when the twins reached the sands below Beaches, there were only a few people about; just one or two locals were walking their dogs. Soon, however, the passenger ferries would be continually picking up passengers in the town and dropping them off at the beach. Families and individuals could then spend the day on the sands, knowing that the ferry was only a few minutes away for their return journey whenever they were ready.

Ellie and Lucy hoped that their grandparents would come down to the beach sometime during the day. They had been going to the local swimming pool with their school, and as their swimming had greatly improved from last year, they were keen to show their grandparents their new skills. They really enjoyed Gramps being on the beach with them. During their previous visits he had organized all sorts of races and games, both in and out of the water, for them and any other people on the beach who wished to join in. Apart from swimming, the twins' favourite activity was beach cricket, and this never failed to interest other beach users.

As the twins feasted their eyes on the water, a yacht passed by in the distance, heading for the harbour, and reminding them of what Gramps had said about smugglers that morning. Lucy, who was a bit of a worrier, asked her sister if she thought that smugglers might sometimes use the harbour to anchor their boats overnight. Ellie just shrugged her shoulders, saying,

"Well, I suppose they might, but I guess it would be a bit risky, as it's such a busy harbour with so many people around." Then, grabbing her sister's hand, she pulled her towards the rocks.

For about two hours they collected shells, some that were open and empty and others that were still closed, along with some unusual rocks, a number of very small crabs, and other small sea creatures to be identified later. Their collections went into their buckets with some sea water. They became totally absorbed with their tasks, until almost 12.30pm, when they decided to return to Beaches. They carried their now-full and very heavy buckets up the steep steps. By the time they had reached the top, they were puffing and panting. They were looking forward to a large glass of juice, which they hoped Gran would have ready for them. They were not disappointed.

In the kitchen, Gramps was sitting in an old armchair next to the Aga cooker, enjoying a cup of tea. When their grandparents' dog had been alive—a gorgeous golden retriever, called Pete, but nicknamed Becks because of his amazing ability with a football—he had always laid in his basket by the side of the cooker. When he died, Gramps moved his chair into the space that was left empty, and now it didn't matter to him whether it was hot or cold outside; he just loved the comfort of sitting in Becks' warm spot.

"Hello, girls. How did your search go this morning?" Gramps asked when he saw the twins.

"Not bad," said Ellie. "We found lots stuff that had been left behind by the tide, but we could only carry up some of it, so we would like to go back down this afternoon, if that's okay. And can we have a swim, too?" they pleaded, giving him a huge smile.

Gramps stroked and pulled his short grey beard and tried to look serious, before finally saying, "I tell you what, girls. I was thinking that an afternoon on the beach might be a good idea, and as it's so hot today, I was fancying a dip myself."

"Me too," joined in Gran. "Going down to the beach, that is, but not swimming. As you know, I never go into the water. No matter how warm you all say the water is, it always feels cold to me," she said with a shudder. "But I do love watching you two girls; you are just like mermaids—so natural—and seeing you in the sea just makes me wish I liked the water more so that I could also keep cool on hot days such as this." Ellie said that they understood how Gran felt and suggested that perhaps she would like to take part in some beach cricket instead. "Perhaps," she laughed. "Although I am in the middle of a good book and wouldn't mind finishing it. So I'm not making any promises."

The decision having been made about the afternoon's activities, Gran suggested that Ellie and Lucy spend time after lunch sorting out their bowl and doing a few drawings. "It's such a hot day," she said, "so it will be best to avoid the midday sun. We can then go down to the beach about three o'clock, if you think that's okay." The girls and Gramps nodded in agreement, and they all sat down at the large kitchen table. With lunch over, Ellie and Lucy went up to their bedroom, taking with them their buckets of shells, seaweed, and other odds and ends.

"I don't know about you," said Ellie to her sister, "but I am absolutely stuffed. If we carry on eating meals like that, we're going to have to do lots of swimming and other exercises—otherwise, we really are going to get big bums!" Laughing, the sisters threw themselves onto their beds and stayed there for a good fifteen minutes. Then, with sufficient rest and their stomachs returned to normal, the twins set about placing the items they had collected in the large bowl that their granddad had already placed on their work table, half filled with sand and sea water. Ellie held a beautiful closed shell in the palm of her hand and asked her sister what she thought of it.

"Ooh, it's so pretty—one of the prettiest shells that I have ever seen, and the markings on it are so unusual . . . I wonder what sort of creature is living inside it!" replied Lucy.

Ellie carefully placed the shell onto a bed of sand and seaweed in the bowl, telling her sister that she was going to try to do a drawing of it.

"Great," responded Lucy, looking intently at the shell, "and whilst you're starting that, I'll go on the laptop and see what I can find. It really is an unusual shell with all those greens and pinks, and so big, too."

Both girls loved anything to do with sea life. Their parents were very interested in marine biology, and so Lucy and Ellie had been raised to love the sea and all that was in it. Most of their holidays with their parents were spent walking on seashores, exploring river beds, as well as drawing and painting the plants and the creatures that lived in the water. They never tired of this, and although too young as yet to make any firm decisions, both felt that they wanted to have some sort of career that involved the sea and everything in it.

Ellie set her sketch book and a box of various coloured pencils on the table in front of the bowl and began her drawing, whilst Lucy busied herself on the laptop. However, despite much searching and looking at hundreds of pictures of shells, she couldn't find anything that resembled the shell in the bowl. Disappointed, she gave up the search and sat at the table with her sister, who had already drawn an outline of the shell and was ready to use colour. They became so involved with their drawings that time passed quickly, and they were surprised when they heard Gran calling them to get ready to go down to the beach.

Chapter 3

After a long swim with Gramps that included races between the three of them, they decided upon a game of beach cricket. As they were setting up the stumps and deciding who would bat first, they were approached by two boys about the twins' age, who asked if they could join in. Their names were Jamie and Ben, and they were on holiday with their parents, who were also on the beach. The boys turned out to be very good at cricket and also very energetic, so Ellie and Lucy did not protest when, after an hour and a half of play, Gran suggested that they call it a day and return to the house for some cold drinks. They said goodbye to the boys, who thanked them for allowing them to join in and added that they had enjoyed themselves so much they would ask their parents if they could return another day. They explained that they would be staying for a few more days at a hotel further along the coast. The girls said that it would be great if they could come again and that they would practice their batting in order to beat them—the boys had played a hard game and knocked spots off the girls, much to Ellie and Lucy's dismay. After they had exchanged mobile numbers and said their goodbyes, the boys and their parents headed for home.

Back at Beaches, the twins took their drinks up to their room, where they wanted to continue their drawings. Ellie sat at the table in front of the glass bowl, whilst Lucy checked her mobile for any messages. There was just one text, from their mum and dad, which she started to read out loud to Ellie, but before she had finished, Ellie interrupted her. She had spotted some movement of the top half of the special shell that they had found.

"Lucy, come and see this, and be quick, or you'll miss it."

"What?"

"Just come over here and look at this. *Ple-e-ease*, hurry up!"

Hearing the urgency in her sister's voice, Lucy was soon by her side and was just in time to see the top of the shell pop open and a tiny creature swim out. Both girls held their breath as the creature swam around the bowl. There looked to be strands of golden hair floating behind the head, and as it came level with Ellie and Lucy's startled faces, it stopped, looked, and then after a few more rounds of the bowl, swam onto one of the rocks and rested on top of it. The creature's lower body was below the water and its head and upper body above.

A quick flick of the golden locks revealed a beautiful face, the face of a girl with bright-green eyes and milk-coloured skin. Her golden hair reached down to her waist, below which was a fish-like tail, covered in green and pink scales which glittered like jewels as it moved in the water.

With both their eyes and mouths wide open, the sisters stared at the tiny creature, the most perfectly formed and beautiful mermaid that they had ever seen. Well, actually, the *only* mermaid they had ever seen. Then the mermaid placed her head in her hands and started to sob. Coming to her senses, and in the smallest voice possible so as not to frighten the creature, and quavering just a little, Ellie said. "P-please don't cry; we are not going to hurt you. M-my s-sister Lucy and I—I'm Ellie by the way—won't harm you."

Raising her head, the tiny sea creature spoke, hiccupping and sobbing as the words tumbled out of her exquisite bow-shaped lips.

"My name is Mia—*hic*—and I have been so silly— *sob, sob*—and I should have been on the beach for my Aunt—*sob*—B to pick me up—*hic*—but I seem to have become trapped in this glass sea garden." Then she placed her head in her cupped hands and sobbed and hiccupped some more.

"We're so, so sorry," gasped Ellie, almost crying herself. Lucy nodded in agreement, and Ellie carried on, "We are responsible for you being in that—that glass sea garden. You see, when we stay with our grandparents—this is their house, by the way—we like to collect shells and other interesting things from the beach. We place them in the glass bowl, the one you are in now, so that we can study and draw what we find. I promise you if we'd known that you were in that shell we would never have disturbed it, although it really is wonderful to meet you."

Lucy just kept nodding, her eyes wide and her mouth slightly open.

"Oh, it's okay," said the mermaid-like creature, now smiling just a little and at the same time stretching her arms out and yawning. "'Scuse me. It's really my own fault that I'm in this mess. You see, the journey here was so tiring. It was very stormy, and the strength of the waves carried me onto the shore earlier than expected. Anyway, I found a large shell that had washed in with me, swam inside, snuggled down, and fell asleep. I shouldn't have done that, but I really was so very tired." She gave another huge exaggerated yawn as if to confirm this. "I knew nothing more until I woke up just a few minutes ago. The lid of the shell had closed down on me and was so tight that I had to push and push as hard as I could to open it. Then I saw that I was no longer in the rock pool but in this glass bowl. I was supposed to stay in the pool until my Aunt B collected me, and now I'm in big, big trouble." Mia lowered her head and once again started to sob and sob.

"Please don't cry," begged Ellie, at the same time thinking that for such a tiny creature Mia certainly made a lot of noise when she cried. In fact, she sobbed so much and so loudly that Ellie fully expected Gran and Gramps to come running into the room to see what was happening. "You really don't need to worry. We will look after you, and perhaps we can contact your Aunt B for you. Is she a mermaid too?"

"Yes . . . and no. You see, we are sea witches . . . it's all quite complicated. I would like to tell you more, but at the moment I am feeling quite claustro— claustrophobic in this glass bowl, and I would like to get out as soon as possible, if you will help me." As she gazed up at Ellie and Lucy, they could see that Mia's large green eyes were now very red and swollen from crying.

Although Ellie and Lucy felt so sorry for Mia and really wanted to make everything better for her, they exchanged looks that clearly indicated they were not sure what they were letting themselves in for. Without taking her eyes off Mia, Ellie reached out and grasped her sister's trembling hand with her own hot and sticky one. Neither of them said anything for a few moments, until Ellie found her voice again and assured Mia that they would do everything they could to help. She told her how sorry they were to have made things difficult by putting her in the bowl. Squeezing her sister's hand, and with a smile that lit up her whole face as the words tumbled out of her mouth, Ellie told Mia how excited she and Lucy were at meeting a mermaid.

"You see," said Ellie, "we have never seen a mermaid before. In fact, we never even knew that they—umm, you know—*existed*, until seeing you, that is. It's so, so— Oh, I can't find the right words! J-just tell us what you want us to do."

"Right," said Mia suddenly sitting upright on the rock, pulling herself together, and taking charge. "This is what we do. I will need you to follow my instructions exactly. Okay?" Ellie and Lucy nodded eager to help. "I would like one of you, when I say so, to scoop up some of the water in this bowl into your cupped hands to allow me to swim into it. You must not under any circumstances let the water drain away. Do you understand?" Both girls nodded that they understood. "When you are holding me safely, I want you to gently place me on the floor and then quickly stand back. As soon as I'm set down, I will cast a spell and, hopefully, I will transform into a girl just like you two, with legs instead of a tail." Ellie and Lucy gasped, but Mia seemed not to notice this and just went on. "I will have to be on the floor with space around me. Can you imagine what it would be like if I changed in the bowl?" She smiled nervously at Ellie and Lucy who, despite their willingness to help Mia, were feeling rather nervous themselves about what was about to happen.

Lucy and Ellie looked at each with worried expressions on their faces. Neither spoke for several seconds, and then Ellie, who was usually the more adventurous of the two sisters, said that she wouldn't mind being the one to lift Mia out of the bowl—unless, of course, Lucy would prefer to do it. She looked at her twin, but Lucy said that she was okay with Ellie doing it. Then Lucy said she would fetch a towel to place on the floor, which would be nicer for Mia and would also prevent Gran wondering what they had been doing if she found a wet carpet. She also suggested that they lock the door, for although Gran rarely came into their room without knocking, it would make them feel more comfortable with what they were about to do.

"Good thinking, Batman," said Ellie. The towel was fetched and placed on the carpet. Checking that Mia was ready, Ellie clasped her hands together and prepared to lower them into the bowl.

Mia looked deeply into Ellie's eyes, shrugged her shoulders and chewed her lower lip. "I hope I get this spell right, as I haven't used it before. I was supposed to cast it when Aunt B collected me from the beach, but I haven't got her here to remind me what to say." She sighed and then in quite an agitated voice said, "Never mind. Let's just do it; I'm sure it will work, as I do have a good memory, and after all, I am a witch and should to be able to sort this blooming mess out." Ellie and Lucy drew in deep breaths as Mia spoke again and looked deep into Ellie's eyes. "Right, on the count of three. Here goes: one, two, three, *go*."

Ellie, with her heart thumping, plunged her shaking hands into the cool sea water whist Lucy looked anxiously on. Mia swam into the water, and Ellie lifted her from the bowl and gently placed her on the towel. Then she quickly moved back to stand by Lucy's side. From the floor rose the sound of Mia's voice, strong and sure:

Mighty sea that has brought me here,
Release the spell that keeps me near.
My mermaid's guise I must now shed,
For on this land I wish to tread.
I will hold dear the sea witch rules,
And spells I've learned I'll not abuse.

Ellie and Lucy did not see what happened next, as it was all over so fast. One minute they were looking and listening as Mia recited her spell, and then— *abracadabra*—in front of them stood another Mia, a girl as tall as them, wearing a pair of light denim cut-offs, a T-shirt to die for, a pair of navy sand shoes, and a very smart watch to top off the outfit. She sported a pair of brown legs and absolutely no sign of a tail! She looked about the same age as the twins, with her blonde hair hanging straight down past her shoulders and a fringe lying along the tops of her eyebrows. Her green eyes were no longer sad but showed her relief at having successfully morphed from mermaid to land girl without a hitch, for if the truth be known, she had been more than a little worried that things might not go as planned!

Chapter 4

Ellie and Lucy stood mesmerized, their lips pouted, their eyes wide. Neither girl moved a muscle. Then Mia spoke.

"Hey, you two, wake up. Sorry to startle you, but it's just me, your friend from the sea," said Mia. She reached out both arms towards Ellie and Lucy, grasping their hands and saying in a very soft voice, "I'm so sorry if I've frightened you, but it was the only way of getting out of that glass bowl. You see, even though I'm a sea witch, I don't have very many powers as yet; Aunt B is going to help me improve these whilst I am staying with her."

Still stunned by what she had just witnessed, Ellie swallowed several times before finally managing to say in a very small voice, "You look great, Mia, and you feel just like us—warm skin and everything—but I just don't know how you managed those clothes . . ." For once in her twelve years, Ellie was unable to find words to express how she was really feeling, while Lucy just continued to stare at Mia, with her mouth slightly open.

Finally Lucy shook herself out of her dream-like state. She let go of the breath she had been holding, and with eyes glistening with excitement, she spoke, the words tumbling out of her mouth. "Those were the longest minutes of my life! I can't believe that you just did that. It's the most awesome thing that I have ever, ever, seen! Can't understand it, but I guess being a witch helped. I've never really believed in mermaids or witches, until now that is. I just thought that they were made up, you know, characters in stories—but you are real, Mia, and I don't want you to go away. It's all so exciting; I can't believe what's happened!" Then turning to her sister with a quizzical look on her face, she asked, "It is real, isn't it Ellie? We really did see a mermaid change into a girl like us?"

But before Ellie could answer, Lucy found her second wind and carried on. "I want to know all about you, Mia—where you live and—" Lucy continued talking non-stop for another minute or so before finally stopping for breath.

Ellie stared at her in amazement; she had never ever heard her sister say so much in one go. Then, taking the opportunity before Lucy could start babbling again, she said, "I feel the same way as Lucy does, Mia, but I can't help worrying about what's going to happen now!"

The twins turned once again to Mia, who had a huge grin on her face. "I realize that I have shocked you, and I do want to explain all about myself, where I come from, and why I am here. But before I do that, I really need to telephone my Aunt B and let her know that I'm okay, although I'm sure that she will already know that I'm safe. You see, she's a senior sea witch, with advanced powers, so she will have been keeping tabs on me. Unfortunately, as I have few powers, I need a phone to make contact to arrange for her to pick me up. Do either of you have a mobile, by any chance? I've had to leave mine at home."

"Yes," chorused Ellie and Lucy, and they rushed to collect their phones. Lucy was the first to find hers, and she thrust the bright-pink mobile towards Mia, saying, "Here you are; use mine. It's already turned on."

Mia thanked Lucy, adding, "It's just like the one I have at home, but I couldn't bring it with me—something to do with water and mobiles not being compatible, whatever that means." She giggled somewhat nervously and then tapped a series of numbers into the phone. Within seconds she was talking to her Aunt.

"Hi, Aunt B . . . yes, I'm fine, thank you . . . so sorry to be such a trouble. I hope you've not been worrying too much." A couple of minutes passed without Mia saying anything, and then she spoke again.

"I know, and I'm so, so sorry. It's all rather complicated, but I'm with two great girls, Ellie and Lucy . . . of course I forgot that you know about them . . . yes, I am quite safe with them." Mia listened to her aunt for a few more minutes with a very thoughtful look on her face. "Their grandparents have no idea that I am in their bedroom, and I feel sure that Ellie and Lucy will not say anything about me and will help me with whatever I need to do, but I will talk to them about it." Again Mia listened to her aunt, with the occasional yes or no in response to whatever her aunt was asking. She continued to listen, although it was clear to the twins from the way she was shuffling her feet and raising her eyes to the ceiling that her aunt was giving her a hard time. Finally she turned to Ellie and Lucy and, shrugging her shoulders, asked them if it was possible to open the bedroom window.

"Yes," responded the twins. Mia passed this on. Turning to the twins again, she raised her eyes to the ceiling and asked them to show her. Lucy and Ellie quickly went over to the window, unlocked it, and pulled the top half down about half a metre.

"This is as far as it will go," said Ellie. "Gramps fixed it like this for safety when we were younger."

Mia passed the information on and listened intently once again for a couple of minutes before speaking. "Yes, Aunt B. I know what I must do, and please don't worry. The twins will help, and I will be fine until you collect me . . . right . . . bye for now. I am really looking forward to seeing you." With that, Mia made a kissing noise into the phone, switched it off, and handed it back to Lucy, thanking her for letting her use it. She then threw herself onto a bed whilst the twins waited in a state of anticipation to hear what was to happen next.

"Okay," said Mia. "Aunt B is unable to get here until later. She says that she will be outside the house on the back road at ten o'clock exactly. She can't get here until then, as she has an exhibition of her paintings at her gallery and must be there for it. Did I tell you that she is a painter and lives in the town across the water?" Ellie and Lucy exchanged wide-eyed looks, and Ellie said that Mia had not mentioned this. "Oh, sorry. I'll tell you more later Anyway, she'd hoped that I would be able to attend the exhibition with her and so isn't best pleased with me for messing things up." Mia pulled a long face before continuing. "I must be standing by an open window when she arrives, because sea witch spells will not work through glass. That's why she wanted you to show me the open window." Mia sighed and carried on. "She said to tell you that she is very grateful for your help and hopes to meet you soon. She also wants me to be absolutely sure that you understand the need for secrecy."

"We do," said Ellie.

"Yes, we really do." added Lucy. Just as they had given Mia their assurances, their gran called out to them to come down for their evening meal.

"Look," said Ellie, "we must go downstairs to eat, but we will be as quick as we can, and when we come back we can talk some more. We shouldn't be too long, as I'm not sure that we'll be able to eat much with all this excitement."

"Definitely," Lucy said as she quickly made her way over to one of the bedside cupboards. She opened the door, reached inside, and pulled out handfuls of wrapped health bars, crisps, apples, and bottles of water, which she placed on top of the bed by Mia. "But perhaps you're hungry, Mia? Mum gave us all of this food to bring with us in case Gran forgot to feed us." She grinned. "As if! Gran feeds us so well that we never need anything extra, so please help yourself to whatever you fancy."

Mia eyed the assortment of goodies. "Thanks, girls. Just what I need." Then, putting a finger up to her mouth, she made a shushing sound. The twins nodded, understanding that Mia was reminding them not to say anything to their grandparents.

By the time the twins had reached the door, Mia had torn the wrapper off one of the bars, and with her mouth full and her eyes shining with pleasure, she waved to the girls as they left the room. Both Ellie and Lucy had the biggest smiles on their faces, for although they would have preferred to stay with Mia, they knew that she would be there for them when they returned. If anyone had asked them how they knew this, they wouldn't have been able to give an answer. They simply trusted that Mia would not let them down.

Chapter 5

Ellie and Lucy always loved their evening meal with their grandparents. Usually there was a constant stream of chatter about the day's events: anything unusual that they had found on the beach, what they were drawing, results of searches on the Internet, and so on. Tonight, however, they were very quiet, both being deep in thought about Mia and anxious to return to their room to make sure that she was still there, even though their instincts told them that she would be. They just needed to see her again, and soon. Finding conversation difficult to keep going, Gran and Gramps looked at each other knowingly before Gran said, "There's a programme on the television tonight that Gramps and I would like to watch, and as you two girls seem rather quiet this evening, perhaps you would like to use the TV in your bedroom, or do whatever pleases you, until you are ready for bed? You can, of course, stay and watch the television with us, if you prefer, and go up when you are ready. It's up to you."

Both girls looked up at their grandmother, and Ellie replied, "That would be great, Gran, going up to our room, I mean. I think we are a little tired, so we'll get into our PJs to watch a bit of TV and—"

Before she had finished, Lucy piped up. "But shall we help you with the dishes first?"

"No, don't worry about that. Gramps will give me a hand; you get off and leave us to it."

The twins hugged their grandparents and headed for the stairs. Opening the bedroom door quietly so as not to frighten Mia, they saw that she was curled up on a bed, fast asleep, her hair spread out on the pillow and surrounded by an assortment of wrappers and empty water bottles. She had such a peaceful look on her face that they hardly dared wake her up. Ellie whispered to Lucy. "What shall we do? Shall we let her sleep, or what?"

"Let's get into our PJs first; then we we'll be ready for bed when Mia has left with her aunt. So we can let her sleep for a few more minutes; she must be so tired after what has happened to her today. I know I would be."

"Okay then," agreed Ellie. "We can be in bed when Gran pops her head around the door as she usually does, about half past ten. Mia should be gone by then." She hesitated and went on, "And fingers crossed that it all works out for her. Can't think what's going to happen if it doesn't." The girls looked at each other with concerned expressions showing on both of their faces. Then they shrugged their shoulders before quietly taking themselves and their PJs into the bathroom.

Five minutes later, the twins were standing by the bed looking down at Mia's sleeping form. Suddenly her eyes opened, making them jump. Seeing the twins, she smiled before sitting up and stretching her arms.

"That sleep was so good, just what I needed." Smiling sheepishly, she pointed at all the food wrappings. "Oh, sorry about the mess, but I was so hungry that I ate and drank just about everything. De-e-e-licious!"

"No probs," piped up the twins whilst silently wondering how one girl/mermaid/witch could eat so many health bars in one go. They always found that one was enough to fill them up, and anyway they didn't taste that great. Ugh! She must have been really hungry.

Mia swung her legs over the end of the bed and said, "Now we know what's going to happen to me at 10 p.m. exactly, we can relax and chat. I'd like know more about you, but I'm sure that tonight you might want to hear a little about me, as I guess what happened earlier must have been a bit scary for you. It certainly was for me." Mia searched the twins' faces for any indication that they were worried or even afraid. Seeing nothing other than interest and anticipation, she continued what she was saying. "I know that you were a bit shocked when I said that I was a witch—well, a sea witch, actually." The twins were nodding in agreement. "Right, first of all I will explain the witch thing. So, shall we get comfy? We can sit on the floor, if you don't mind, as one bed's not really big enough for all three of us." With that, Lucy pulled the duvets off both beds, laid them on the floor, and then threw the pillows on top. The threesome then plonked down and made themselves comfortable.

"Firstly," began Mia, attempting to look serious, "I must have your absolute promise that you will speak to no one about what you have already seen today or about what you are going to hear and see tonight. Aunt Bella has asked me to make sure that you understand that it all must be kept a secret." The twins were nodding to show that they understood. "You see, Aunt B has the power to place a 'forgetting' spell on you both so that you won't remember what's gone on today, but she said that she is prepared to accept my word that you can be trusted." Again the twins nodded, their faces serious, and Mia carried on. "I would like to have you as true friends, and that means being able to talk to you about my life under the sea—you know, about school, my friends and, of course, my family. The same as I want to hear all of those same those things about you."

Ellie was the first to respond to Mia. "I'm speaking for me and Lucy. We really can be trusted. We are very good at keeping secrets, and so if our friendship with you means we have to keep things to ourselves, then we will. In a way, it's easier for us to keep secrets than it is for most people. You see, we know absolutely everything about each other, and we always seem to know what the other is thinking, I guess it's something to do with us being identical twins. Because of this, we really trust each other and have no need to share our thoughts, feelings, or secrets for that matter, with anyone else. Unless we really want to, that is." She looked deep into Mia's eyes before finishing. "We have only known you for a short time, but it feels like we have always known you—you know, just like me and Lucy have always known each other. So, Mia, please convince your aunt that your secrets are safe with us." She put her arm around her sister.

"Right, what do you want to know?" said Mia with a smile.

"Absolutely everything," came the twins' insistent reply as they settled back onto the pillows and prepared to listen.

"Just like on land," Mia began, "life developed in the seas many, many hundreds of thousands of years ago. Of course, I don't know everything about all our history, just what I have learned at school about the life and development of mermaids and sea witches. You see, mermaids have lived in the oceans as long as man has lived on the land. We have always been kind and gentle and prepared to help others, especially those in trouble at sea." The twins nodded, and Mia continued, "Well, eventually mermaids—and by the way, I also mean mermen—grew legs, just like land people, but kept tails to swim like fish. They built shelters to shut out the sea and dangerous creatures. Over thousands and thousands of years these shelters became houses, and the houses became towns and cities. Then, at some point, and nobody knows exactly how or why, my people developed powers of mind over matter. *Spells* to you and me, a mixture of thoughts and words, although sometimes it's just thoughts that can make things happen. Some say we developed this way in order to survive and defeat the predators, and believe me, some of those are so huge and vicious even in this modern time. They would eat you alive just like that!" Mia snapped her fingers to emphasize this. All three girls shuddered at the same time. Mia continued, "That is why, when we travel the oceans we are protected by an invisible shield. No sea creature, large or small, would dare to approach us, as to do so would mean their destruction. Once we are in a safe place and don't need the protection, the shield just disappears. We are then able to use special spells to enable us to change back to our normal size. As you know, when you first saw me I was very tiny. This was because I had been travelling and had fallen asleep before I could change, and . . . well, you know the rest." Mia laughed nervously. She knew how close she had come to disaster because of her laziness and how lucky she had been that it was the twins who had found her. "In my homeland, of course, I am as big as I am now."

The twins sat spellbound as Mia continued to tell the most interesting story that they had ever heard or read about—as keen readers they had read many books.

Mia stretched her arms above her head, giving a large yawn. "Are you sure you want me to go on?" she asked.

"Oh yes, please," replied Ellie, whilst Lucy just nodded, unable to take her eyes off Mia.

"Well, here goes. At some point in our history, sailors believed that mermaids were dangerous creatures that could cause their boats to capsize and that this was likely to happen if they heard a mermaid's song. No one knew if this was true or not. Actually, we are just like you—some of us have good singing voices and some of us don't. I can't carry a tune to save my life; it would frighten sailors away if they heard it!" Ellie and Lucy giggled as Mia paused for breath. "My people eventually became sea witches with special powers. Some became curious about life above the sea; they were permitted to swim up to the surface and even go onto land to watch the world above. Over time, some fell in love with land men or women and were even prepared to give up their lives in the sea to pursue this love or even just to find out about this other land. However, once they had made this choice, they were not allowed to return."

"That's such a wonderful story, but it's also a rather sad one, too," said Lucy with a sigh.

"It certainly is," added Ellie, "but more important, what will happen to you, Mia? Will you have to stay here? Oh, I really hope so—if you don't mind me saying that?" she added sheepishly.

"Oh, I don't mind, and it's nice of you, but I'll probably go back with my parents, unless they decide not to. Anyway, what I've told you was a long, long time ago. Things have changed since then. Of course, we still have rules about travel outside of our own world but not such strict ones. My Aunt B, for example, has chosen to live on land to paint. She's a wonderful artist. On one of her first visits to Devon several years ago, she started landscape painting and found that she was very good at it. She then went to college to study art and now has chosen to settle in Devon. Whether she returns to the sea to actually live there will now be her decision, but if she does choose to continue living here, she will not be prevented from visiting her family and friends or even returning to her life there."

"Do many people choose to live on land?" asked Lucy.

"Quite a few, but you would never know who they are. They are usually people who have come here to attend college or university and then will return home."

Realizing that she had been talking for quite some time Mia glanced at her watch. Seeing that it was a quarter to ten, she told the twins that they must prepare for Aunt B's arrival. She added that she had made a mental note of Lucy's mobile number when they were downstairs having supper and would call them when she was safely with her aunt, and also the next morning to arrange to meet up on the beach.

"That would be good, wouldn't it, Lucy?" asked Ellie, giving her sister a prod to bring her back to the present.

Lucy jumped and nodded, saying, "Okay then, let's open the window for Mia."

Mia hugged the girls in turn and reassured them that she would be okay, before she turned to face the open window. Ellie couldn't help but think how beautiful she looked.

As Ellie looked at her own watch she saw that it was almost ten o'clock. She raised her eyes to look at Mia, and in a blink, Mia was gone. Even Lucy, who had not taken her eyes off their new friend, did not see anything. One second Mia was there and then she wasn't. Holding hands, the sisters walked to the window; they could see nothing but the white crests of the waves on the water and the lights of the town opposite twinkling like stars in the distance. They closed the window, turned, and walked to their beds in silence, each dragging a duvet and pillow back to her bed. They snuggled under the covers, and before they could say a word to each other, Lucy's mobile vibrated on the side table. She quickly reached for it.

A now-familiar voice greeted her, and she pressed a button to increase the sound so Ellie could also hear the call. Mia's voice filled the room.

"Hi, Ellie and Lucy. I'm safe and sound here with Aunt B. She says to say hello and looks forward to meeting you both tomorrow. I'll call you again in the morning. Talk soon, and sleep tight." The call ended, and Ellie and Lucy smiled at each other. Lucy switched off the side light, and both girls settled down to think about all that had happened that day. When their grandmother popped her head around the door, she found her granddaughters fast asleep.

Chapter 6

The morning after their magical encounter with Mia, the twins woke up to brilliant sunshine streaming through the large window of their bedroom. They dragged themselves out of bed and into the bathroom to get ready for the day ahead, whatever it might provide. Lucy hoped to influence what was going to happen by crossing her fingers. Ellie saw what Lucy was doing, and Lucy, seeing that her twin had noticed, looked at her, shrugged, sighed, and said, "Well, it's always worth trying." Ellie just smiled and held both of her hands up for Lucy to see her own crossed fingers. After all, they had both thought, if mermaids or sea witches were real and could do magical things, then maybe crossed fingers could make their wishes come true. Anyway, it wouldn't hurt to try!

Showered and with their teeth brushed, the twins dressed in beach clothes and were about to go down for breakfast when Lucy's phone vibrated in the pocket of her shorts. Eagerly pulling it out, she saw that it was

Mia's Aunt B's number, and she took the call, once again increasing the sound for Ellie to hear.

Mia's excited voice was soon to be heard chatting away with plans for meeting up on the beach later that morning with Aunt B, who wanted to be introduced to the twins. Mia went on to explain that as it was such a lovely day her aunt was going to bring her painting equipment with her, so that she could work on the beach for a few hours. Her exhibition which had opened the previous evening, the one that Mia had missed, had been so successful that her aunt felt it necessary to start producing some more paintings to replace the ones that had been sold. Lucy told her that they planned to be on the beach most of the day so would keep an eye on the ferry for their arrival. Ending the call, Lucy turned to her sister with a satisfied look, and said, "I wondered when I woke up this morning if I had just been dreaming, but as soon as I heard Mia's voice on the phone, I knew it was all real."

"Same with me," Ellie replied. Before they could talk any more about their plans for the day ahead, Gran called them for breakfast.

It was midmorning when Mia arrived at the beach with her aunt, having come across on the estuary ferry. As the twins watched their arrival, they clutched each other's trembling hands, their knees knocking, their mouths dry, and perspiration forming on their brows. Mia, seeing that the twins were nervous, drew them into a hug before introducing them to her aunt. She whispered, "Don't be afraid; it's only Aunt B."

They looked up in awe at the tall, slender woman whose golden hair and green eyes exactly matched Mia's. To say the least, they had been rather worried about meeting her—after all she was a witch—but they immediately felt very comfortable, and all their fear disappeared when she held a hand out to each of them. In a whispery voice that sounded like tinkling bells, she thanked them for all the help that they had given her niece the previous day.

Aunt B's eyes seemed to penetrate their very being as she said, "My niece assures me that you can be totally trusted, and having met you I believe what she has said, so I don't think I need to cast a forgetting spell on you." Ellie and Lucy smiled nervously, and Mia's aunt continued, "I hope that you two girls and Mia will spend a lot of time together over the next few weeks and become good friends during your holiday. Mia has a lot to learn about life on land, and I think that time spent with you both will help her to achieve this. What do you think?" she asked, looking at them intently. Ellie's mouth was very dry, but she managed to find her voice to reply.

"Oh yes, we already feel like Mia is our friend, and we'd like to spend time with her." Lucy nodded in agreement and managed to smile whilst swallowing hard. Releasing their hands, Aunt B said that she was going to find a shady place to do her painting.

Ellie, Lucy, and Mia watched her as she walked towards the shelter of the cliffs. There she set up her easel and opened up the small collapsible table and canvas chair that she'd brought with her, moving them all around until their positions suited her. When she was happy with what she had arranged, she delved into a large, colourful beach bag and brought out an assortment of paint boxes, an amazing number of brushes, bottles of water, a collection of rags, and a box of tissues. Placing these on the table, she again dug into her bag, this time lifting out a large pad which she placed on the easel. The twins were amazed at the number of things that Aunt B had pulled out of her bag. They breathed a sigh of relief when they saw that she had finished and was finally starting to paint.

With Aunt B settled, the three friends went off to explore the beach and rock pools, whilst at the same time finding out a little more about each other, their families and their different lifestyles, and bonding in a way that others might not understand given the short amount of time that they had known each other.

The twins learned that Mia had just celebrated her twelfth birthday and had a brother named Gi, who was almost eighteen.

"What's your brother like? Is he good-looking?" asked Ellie, blushing.

"Well, he's tall and muscular 'cos he works out a lot. He has blond hair just a bit darker than mine. *And* he teases me."

Lucy, to her sister's amazement, said, "He sounds dishy. Do you have a picture of him?"

"Afraid not," Mia laughingly replied. "Actually, he's in Europe at the moment. Mum and Dad have allowed him to go off with a friend who is going to university with him; they start at Oxford in September. They began their holiday in France about ten days ago and are going to work their way around France, then Italy, Germany, and a few other countries before ending up here."

"Hope we meet them," said Ellie, to which Mia replied that she would see what she could do if they arrived before Ellie and Lucy had returned home.

"If you miss them, I will send you a snap of them," she promised. "Mum and Dad are also abroad; they are in Switzerland attending a conference at the moment, which is why I am staying with Aunt B."

"It's really weird," said Lucy, tilting her head to one side and looking thoughtful. "Our mum and dad are also in Switzerland, at a doctors' conference. I don't suppose that your parents are doctors, like ours, are they?" When Mia nodded, Lucy spluttered, "I bet it's the same conference that our parents are attending. It's like all this was meant to be . . . to happen . . . that we were meant to meet up." Ellie and Mia nodded in agreement; they had been thinking exactly the same thing.

"Will you tell us some more about your home, Mia? That's if you don't mind?" asked Ellie.

"Sure," replied Mia, "as long as you're not bored with hearing me talk."

"Never!" came the joint cry. During the next twenty minutes or so, the twins learned that Mia lived in a city called Shellamac, which was just one of many cities under the seas and oceans that were linked by water tunnels, which allowed the sea people to travel safely using their fish tails. Once inside the cities, they were able to walk about with legs and feet just as people did on dry land. There were roads for cars within the cities, and larger cities also had train systems. Everything worked with electricity. Houses were constructed of bricks made from crushed shells of many colours, which gave off lots of light that compensated for not having any direct sunlight.

As Mia continued with her description of the city where she lived with her parents and brother, the twins also learned that she had grandparents, several aunties and uncles, many cousins, and lots of friends. They were totally absorbed in Mia's description of her life and had begun to gain an understanding of the similarities and differences between her life under the sea and their own life on land. And so the morning passed with Mia, Ellie, and Lucy engrossed in learning about each other.

At round eleven thirty, the twins' grandfather came down to the beach, wearing shorts and sandals and carrying his folding chair and newspaper. He settled down and looked along the beach for his granddaughters. He squinted a little against the brightness of the sun and spotted them quite some distance away, sitting on top of the group of rocks that formed the small pools that the twins liked to explore. He waved to them and held up the large bottle of juice that he had brought down with him. He saw that they had another girl with them, whose hair shone like gold in the sun. As all three were in deep conversation, he thought to himself that they would no doubt come over when they were ready.

Gramps had settled down to read his paper when he spotted a woman to his right with an easel in front of her, whom he recognized as Bella Beason, the owner of the art gallery in the centre of the town. He and his wife had attended an exhibition of her work before Christmas the previous year and had bought one of her paintings that they had fallen in love with. The painting showed their house sitting on the cliffs, with the winter's sea below. It now hung above the fireplace in their living room.

Delighted to see the artist again, he walked over to her and introduced himself, explaining that he and his wife had bought one of her pictures. She laid her brush down and shook his hand, saying, "Oh yes, I remember you and the painting that you bought. It's so good to meet you again." Aunt B never forgot any of her paintings and who had purchased them. Her witchery also meant that she was aware of his relationship to Ellie and Lucy, but she nevertheless asked him if he was by any chance the grandfather of the twin girls who were with her niece. She pointed to where the three girls were sitting, deeply engrossed in conversation.

"Yes, the twins are staying with me and their grandmother and will be here for three weeks."

"My niece is also staying with me for three weeks, in my flat above my studio in the town; she arrived yesterday. It's her first visit, so I'm pleased to see that she has already made friends. She loves the beach and swimming, so I'm sure she is going to be spending a great deal of time on this side of the estuary."

Just as she'd finished speaking, the three girls arrived, and Aunt B introduced Mia to the twins' grandfather, who offered the three girls glasses of the juice. They all accepted and sat down together on a large beach towel.

"My goodness, you would think that the girls had known each other forever, the way they are with each other," said Gramps. Mia's aunt nodded in agreement. "Look," he continued, "why don't you and Mia come up to the house and have lunch with us later? It will just be sandwiches, but my wife always makes far too many, and she would be pleased to see you again and meet Mia." Aunt B said that lunch would be lovely and asked if it would be okay for her to take her painting gear up to the house with her.

About an hour later, Aunt B had done as much as she could to her painting and decided that she would finish it in her studio. Everyone gathered together their personal belongings and headed up the steps to the house. Introductions were made to Gran, who didn't mind having two extra people for lunch. She was always ready to welcome people into her home and was particularly pleased to meet the artist who had painted her favourite picture. They all sat out in the garden around a big old table that was sheltered from the sun by a number of tall trees, and they were soon tucking into sandwiches and cakes. No one spoke for a few minutes.

Once they began to talk, it became apparent that Aunt B and the twins' grandparents were going to get along famously, and much to the three girls' delight, arrangements were soon being made for Mia to take the ferry over to the beach each morning to spend time with Ellie and Lucy. Gran and Gramps had promised to look after her as if she were one of their own family. Aunt B was pleased with this arrangement, saying that it would allow her to be at the gallery most mornings and spend time with her niece in the afternoons. It was also agreed that the girls could have sleepovers at both homes, should they want to do this.

The girls looked and listened in amazement. As the grownups seemed to like each other so much, it was not going to be a problem for them to spend lots and lots of time together. When they were out of earshot, with a smile and a wink, Mia said, "It's almost as if someone has cast a happy spell."

At the other end of the garden, where the grownups were still sitting, Gran said, "Look at those girls!

They are getting on so well, I think there must be something in the air." Gramps nodded whilst Aunt B gave one of her enchanting smiles, her eyes sparkling with amusement. Ellie, Lucy, and Mia smiled at the grownups and set about making plans for the days ahead. They were thinking to themselves that this was going to be a fantastic holiday.

Chapter 7

The days following the meeting between Aunt B, Gran, and Gramps just flew by. The three girls spent the best part of each day in one another's company. If the weather was good, sometimes Gramps and Gran would come to the beach with them, or Aunt B would be there working on a painting. They had sleepovers at each other's holiday homes. When the weather was poor, they spent time indoors drawing, reading, and talking.

Mia spent some of her holiday increasing her knowledge of witch spells, under her aunt's tuition. Aunt B one of the most learned of sea witches, and she had spent several years in the city of Shellamac tutoring young sea witches in the practice of spells. It was considered dangerous for them to leave their own world without this knowledge. They needed the spells to cope with different situations that they might have to face. Mia's parents had already taught her sufficient spells to enable her to travel from Shellamac to Devon, where she was fortunate to have an aunt to help her with any difficulties. Others were not so fortunate. She now had to increase her knowledge with her aunt's help.

Every new spell that Mia learned she demonstrated for the twins. They squealed with delight when she practiced the first one. This allowed her to move about the room from corner to corner at such lightning speed that the twins were unable to see her move. The spell, she explained to them, was used for getting out of dangerous or just difficult situations, such as the one she had been in when Aunt B had had to remove her from their bedroom. Had Mia known it then, she could have gotten out of the mess by herself.

"I wish I could do what you've just done," said Lucy wistfully. "It would be great for avoiding the bullies at school." Tears welled up in her eyes as she remembered the girls who had bullied her the previous year. At first the bullies had picked on both Ellie and Lucy, making fun of them because they were identical. When they got bored with just teasing, they'd forced Lucy to help them with homework projects, picking on her because of the high grades she received. Lucy had said nothing about this for fear that they might pick on Ellie as well, but they'd chosen to bully another bright girl. When Lucy could not cope any more, she'd confided in one of her schoolmates, who had gone with her to report the bullies.

"Yeah, it would be really cool," said Ellie, with eyes as big as saucers. "Can you imagine the looks on their faces when we just disappeared? They would be standing there shouting at themselves and looking like the idiots they are." At the thought of this, all three girls laughed until their sides ached, and Lucy wiped her wet cheeks.

When they had recovered, Mia looked thoughtful. With her eyes twinkling and her voice full of excitement, she asked, "Wouldn't it be great if we could all go to the same school? We would have such a good time, and you would never be bullied if I was around, although I would have to improve on my magical powers first—otherwise those bullies might be turned into toads by mistake!" They all laughed again, with the twins nodding, their expressions speaking for them. If only . . .

On the Friday of the first week of their holiday, the twins received an unexpected mobile call from the two boys who had joined them for beach cricket on their second day with Gran and Gramps. Jamie and Ben asked if Ellie and Lucy would be on the beach that afternoon, as they were going to be there with their parents. The twins told them where they would be and that they would have another friend with them.

When the boys arrived as arranged and were introduced to Mia, they were initially dumbstruck by her looks and then, quickly pulling themselves together, they got down to what they were there for.

"Shall we set up to play cricket?" asked Ben. "We've brought our stumps and bats. Mum and Dad have them," he said, pointing to a couple who were sitting on a blanket further along on the beach.

"Great," shouted the others in unison.

"But there are now three girls", said Jamie, "and just two boys."

"Great powers of observation bro," teased Ben.

"It'll be okay," Ellie responded, laughing. "Our granddad will be coming down soon. He loves cricket, so we can ask him if he will play for your team."

When Gramps arrived, he readily agreed. Seeing Gramps' arrival, the boys' father, John, went over to say hello and to offer his help. Gramps told him that he was going to join the boys but that both teams could use a wicket keeper.

The boys won the toss, and the girls decided that Lucy should go in to bowl first. Jamie was the first of his team to bat and he scored several runs, being cheered on loudly by his mother, Lisa, who had now been joined by Gran. Ellie was second bowler, and again runs were added to the boys' score. Mia took her turn, and she bowled Jamie out with her third ball. The boys looked on in amazement. Such was the speed of Mia's bowling that the poor boy had not seen the ball coming. The girls threw their sun hats in the air and shouted with delight, along with Gran. Next, Ben was in to bat, and he scored just three runs before Mia bowled him out too. Again the girls whooped with joy. Gramps took the bat and laughingly said that he was glad Mia had already bowled. Gramps was pretty good at cricket, and he gained several runs. Then it was Mia's turn to bowl again. Gramps scored four runs before he was out. The boys were gracious enough to clap. Ellie and Lucy looked at each other with lips slightly turned up into knowing smiles.

After a short break with team huddles, it was the girls' turn to bat. Mia had assured the twins that her bowling had been straight, with no witchery involved. Then, with a giggle, she said, "Of course, it always helps to have very good vision, something that I was born with. Poor boys! I really did try to be gentle with them, but I reckoned your granddad was man enough to take it. Next round, though, when I'm bowling, I'll be a little gentler with him, too." Giggling, Mia, Ellie, and Lucy returned to the game.

Ellie and Lucy each batted well but didn't quite match the boys' score before being bowled out. Then it was Mia's turn to bat, and whoever was bowling from the boys' team, she just kept hitting the ball and gaining run after run. When the agreed playing time for the first half of the match was over, they had a drinks break. Everyone was pleased to have a rest, as it was an extremely hot day.

During the rest period, the boys asked Mia how she came to be so good at cricket, and she told them how her older brother was cricket captain at his school and that he had taught her to play. "Well," said Jamie, "I just hope that I never have to play against him; it's bad enough playing against his sister!" Everyone laughed. After all, it was just a game.

After the break, when it was Mia's turn to bowl, she took it a little easier on the opposite team. Nevertheless, when all the runs from the two halves of the match were added up, John declared the girls to be the winners and asked for three cheers from the boys. Gramps, whilst very pleased for his granddaughters and Mia, was a little mystified as to how they had beaten the boys' team by ten runs! And he had thought at the start of the game that maybe, to be fair on the girls, the teams should be mixed! Chuckling to himself, he thought: Next time I am going to have Mia on my side!

For the rest of the afternoon, whilst the adults chatted and shared a flask of tea, the five friends went swimming and arranged races. Mia, of course, proved to be impossible to beat. Poor Mia, however hard she tried to lose, she found herself at the front of whoever she was racing against. After she beat Jamie, who was himself a very good swimmer, he laughingly and breathlessly asked her whether her brother also headed up the swimming team at their school and had taught her how to swim.

"No, it's just one of those things," Mia replied. "We are both natural swimmers, although my brother is a much better swimmer than me, as he's bigger and stronger." She went on to apologize, saying, "I'm so sorry if I'm a bit of a pain. I'm not showing off, you know; it's just that I'm a good athlete, and when I'm involved in these activities I can't seem to hold back."

"Hey, don't apologize," Jamie quickly responded, giving Mia's shoulder a soft pat. Then, blushing and stuttering a little, he added, "I—I mean *we*," looking at his brother for support, "think you're great—well, I mean, you're all great, and we wish we could come and spend more time with you all, but we have to go home, so . . ." Jamie held his hands up and shrugged.

"That's a shame," said Ellie, while Lucy and Mia nodded in agreement.

"Yep," joined in Ben, "we were supposed to be here another couple of days, but Dad's got to return to work. You see, he's manager at a marina where we live in Suffolk, and a yacht that had been moored up in there for a few days has been stopped and searched by Customs officers and police, and lots of drugs have been found. Dad feels he must go back to support his staff, as the police will be interviewing everyone, collecting information. We're lucky to have stayed today. Mum's got everything packed, and we are off about six this evening to avoid heavy traffic the other end of the journey. So it's bye for now and thanks, girls, for a great day."

"Me too," added Jamie, handing over a list of his and Ben's phone numbers, email addresses, and Facebook details. "Keep in touch," he called over his shoulder as he and his brother joined their parents and headed for their car, ready to start their journey home.

Shortly after Jamie and Ben had left, the twins waved Mia off on the next ferry.

Chapter 8

The next morning, Mia arrived at the beach with a large bag, prepared for a two-night sleepover at Beaches, as arranged between her aunt and the twins' grandparents. The first thing they did was to head up to the bedroom to drop off Mia's bag. Throwing herself across a bed, Mia said, "I don't know about you two, but I'm totally shattered and not really up for much today. Last night I had to go with Aunt B to yet another open evening. Took us about an hour to get there. We stayed about two hours and then went home again. It was mind-blowingly boring, and I've seen enough paintings to last me forever." Then, as an afterthought, she added, "The eats were good, though. There were these yummy round cake things, covered in sugar, with jam in the middle—called doughnuts, although there were no nuts in them. I just love the food here." Stopping for breath, she suggested that they have a lazy morning, to which the twins readily agreed.

They took their time before going to the beach, spending the morning reading and drawing and talking about the previous day's cricket match with Jamie and Ben and how great it had been to beat them. Lucy, however, was thinking of other things. When the boys had told them the reason for cutting short their holiday, her tummy had done a funny flip as she remembered Gramps mentioning smuggling a few days earlier. She hadn't said anything to Ellie after the boys and Mia had left, and she was not going to mention it now, as she didn't want to break the promise that she had made to herself to stop being a wimp.

Ever since being bullied at school, Lucy had lost her self-confidence. She didn't chatter as much as she used to and often let Ellie speak for her rather than voice her own feelings and opinions. At school she stayed close to her sister as much as she could, but even Ellie got frustrated with her occasionally and told her to grow up. Since Mia had arrived in her life, she had begun to feel like her old self again, and she didn't want anything to spoil it. However, her vivid imagination—which was great when writing stories, at which she excelled—did sometimes get the better of her.

After the three friends had finished their lunch and played a game of Scrabble, they were ready to go down to the beach. As it was again a lovely sunny day, they were soon out of their T-shirts and shorts and into their swimming gear. They sat on the edge of the sand with their feet in the warm water, allowing the small waves to lap over them. However tired they might have felt before, they didn't stop talking—that is, until Mia jumped to her feet, ran into the sea, and swam away into the deeper water. All that the twins could see was a slight movement as Mia's body swiftly and smoothly moved further away from them. They gripped each other's hands and looked around to see if Gramps was in his usual place on the beach. Their first thought was to call him, for although Mia was a fantastic swimmer, she had given no explanation as to what she was about, and they were concerned for her. Unfortunately, Gramps had not yet made his way down to the beach. The girls looked at each other, panic showing on both of their faces. They cast their eyes back to the sea just in time to see Mia plucking something out of the water and starting to swim back to shore. Only then were they able to release the breath each had been holding.

As she reached the shallow water, Mia stood up, still clutching a white bundle. The twins waded out to meet her and saw that Mia had a small, wet, bedraggled, white-furred animal in her arms.

"Oh, Mia, you've rescued a little dog," gasped Ellie.

"You're so brave," added Lucy, "but how on earth did you see it?" Before Mia could answer her, Lucy had taken the dog from Mia, clutched it close to her, and led the way back up to where they had left their belongings. By the time they had reached their beach bags, Gramps had arrived. Lucy quickly explained what had happened. He listened; then turning to Mia, who was busy using a towel to squeeze the water from her hair, checked that she was okay. He took the dog from Lucy, wrapped it in another towel, and said that it would be best if they all returned to Beaches to sort out the dog issue.

As soon as Gran saw the dog, she bustled around to see to its needs. Then she fetched drinks and biscuits for the girls and Gramps, as well as a few pieces of chicken, left over from the previous night's meal, for the dog. Although still looking rather sad and bedraggled, the dog perked up when he saw the chicken and did not have any problem eating it all. After another drink of water, the dog gave itself a good shake and jumped up onto Mia's lap.

"Well, he certainly knows who saved him," said Gramps, chuckling. "I guess you have made a friend for life there, but you know, Mia, you really should not have swum out into the deep water. You could have been in trouble yourself. I know that you are a very good swimmer, but I hope that this is the one and only time that you will break the rules. We promised your aunt that we would look after you, and we intend to do just that."

"I promise," replied Mia. "It's just that—"

"No excuses please, Mia—just the promise will do," said Gramps in his deep voice and trying to look stern.

This was Mia's first contact with a real dog. She had seen many pictures of dogs and other animals on the Internet, but in her city they did not have dogs. They had cats, plenty of them, most of them black. Although she was a little bit uneasy about being so close to this land creature, she gave the dog a cuddle. While rubbing her hand over it's fur, she felt a collar with a metal object attached. Gramps saw what she had found and said, "Looks like that's an identity disc. Let's see if it will give us an idea of who this little chap belongs to." On one side of the disc, the name *Bertie* was engraved, and on the reverse was a mobile phone number. When Gramps said, "Bertie," the little dog sat up on Mia's lap and looked alert. Mia stroked his still-damp fur, telling him that he was safe and would soon be returning home. As if he had fully understood what she was saying, Bertie gave a little "Woof, woof," licked Mia's face, and settled down once again on her lap. Gran smiled at the dog's response and said that she would go back indoors, call the number on the landline, and hopefully make arrangements for the owners of

Bertie to pick him up. "Not that I want him to go, as I rather like the little dog. I've quite missed having a dog around since our Becks died. Gramps and I often talk about having another one but . . ." then she went off to make the call.

Whilst Gran was indoors, Gramps and the girls sat with Bertie, who had gone to sleep on Mia's lap. They were trying to guess what breed of dog he was. They all took guesses and then eventually decided that it was a bichon frise. Lucy was the one who guessed this, as one of their friends had a similar dog.

After about ten minutes, Gran returned. "Well, firstly," she said, "I spoke to a woman called Sandy. Let's see, now. Bertie belongs to Sandy and Mark, who come from Plymouth but are staying in a holiday cottage called Overlook, just up the hill from us, about a five-minute walk. They've rented for a month and have already been there for two and a half weeks." She paused before continuing. "It seems that Sandy was on a yacht which was moored in the marina. She was with a girlfriend, and they had secured Bertie with a rope to a post in one of the cabins and left the door open for him so he would not feel shut in, but in the half hour that they were looking around the yacht Bertie had managed to chew through the rope!" Everyone looked at Bertie, who just snuggled down some more on Mia's lap. "They searched everywhere for him and even used binoculars to scan the water. They couldn't see him and so called the harbour master's office to report their loss, hoping that someone might find him and report it in. Sandy has been devastated and was still crying as I was talking to her. She is so relieved and grateful that Bertie has been found." Gran paused whilst the girls stroked Bertie and Mia told him that he would soon be going home. He gave a small yelp, and his tail thumped against Mia's hand.

Gran continued, telling the group about the arrangements that had been made for Bertie's collection. It seemed that Sandy's husband, Mark, and her friend's partner were work colleagues and although on holiday, they had to attend an all-day meeting in Plymouth so would not be back until about seven o'clock that evening, with Sandy and Mark's car. Gran had assured Sandy that Bertie was fine and that it would be all right for them to collect him later.

"Yippee!" shouted the three girls simultaneously.

"Right," said Gran, "if one of you girls comes and helps me in the kitchen, we can prepare for an early meal so that we are ready when Bertie's owners arrive." Ellie jumped up to offer her services, and together they headed for the kitchen.

By seven o'clock, all the food had been eaten, the table cleared, and the dishes washed, courtesy of Gramps, Mia, and Lucy. Everyone settled in the living room with Bertie. He was such a friendly dog and didn't seem to be at all disturbed by his traumatic adventure. Now he lay on Mia's lap, with his head on his paws, intent upon having a little snooze and unconcerned with what was going on around him. However, he had only managed to close his eyes for about five minutes when the front doorbell rang. Up he jumped, with his head on one side, and gave several short yaps, almost as if he knew who was at the door. When he saw Sandy and Mark walking into the room, he bounced with joy on his little legs before quickly returning to the comfort of Mia's lap.

Chapter 9

Sandy was much shorter than her husband, casually dressed, and had long, unruly, light-blonde hair. Mark, who was smartly dressed, wore his dark-brown hair cut in a modern short style. Mia couldn't help thinking that as a couple they really didn't go together.

After giving Bertie a huge hug and being covered with kisses, Sandy thanked everyone for what they had done for Bertie. Mark added his thanks and said that Bertie was really Sandy's sister's dog, and they were just looking after him whilst she was in hospital, as she hadn't wanted to put him in kennels. Gramps explained how it was Mia who had rescued Bertie. Sandy said that she couldn't thank Mia enough and that she was grateful to all of them for taking care of him, adding that she could see how contented Bertie was in their company.

Sandy, Mark, and Bertie were at the front door, ready to leave, when Sandy turned to the girls, all of whom had sad expressions at the thought of saying farewell to Bertie.

"If by any chance you are at a loose end and would like to take Bertie for a walk, then please just give me a call on the number that your grandmother used to contact me. I have a feeling that Bertie would love to spend more time with you." She then turned to Gran and Gramps, saying, "That is, of course, if you both agree."

Gramps smiled and said, "I know that we would all love to see Bertie again. In just the few hours that we've known the little chap we have become very attached to him. Seeing him again would please us all, I'm sure." Everyone else was nodding in agreement.

"How about tomorrow afternoon, then?" suggested Ellie hopefully. "Lucy, Mia, and I could walk up to your house after lunch. Then we could bring Bertie to see Gran and Gramps before taking him onto the beach. We will watch him very carefully. I promise not to let anything bad happen to him."

"Bertie's safety is the last thing that I would be worried about in your company," replied Sandy. "I'm sure that you would be great chaperones and spoil him silly." And wear him out, she secretly thought. "It will suit me just fine, as I have a lot of work to do at home after losing time today. You see, Mark and I work for the same firm and have brought our computers with us. We have rented the house for a whole month, so we can enjoy being by the sea but also give time to a rather important work project. We hope to complete our work by the end of this week and then have a few days to just relax and spend time on the beach—that is, if the sun continues to shine."

"I'm sure it will," Gran assured her. "The weather forecast is good for the next two weeks. There may be the odd cooler day, but generally, on this part of the coast it is warm and sunny well into autumn. We moved here when we retired because we love the area but also because of the warmer climate."

"That all sounds so positive," responded Sandy. "It's a beautiful place." Then, turning to the girls, she said. "I look forward to seeing you all tomorrow afternoon. I've got one of those extendable leads so Bernie can explore a bit more without running off. On the whole, though, I find Bertie to be a very obedient dog; one firm word usually does the trick." The three girls were listening intently. Finally Sandy told them that she would have a bag of his doggy treats ready to take with them. Sandy stood up and finished by saying, "I guess we'd better take Bertie home now. I expect that he is quite tired after all that has happened to him today. It's been lovely meeting you all, and I look forward to seeing you girls again tomorrow."

"Good to have met you, too," spoke up Gramps. "I may well just walk with the girls to your house tomorrow, so my wife and I will know exactly where they are. Just one of our safety measures whilst we are in charge of them. After that, if all goes well, they can collect Bertie on their own any time that you want a little time to yourself."

"Great—an excellent idea! I'll see you tomorrow, then," said Sandy. As she leaned forward to pick Bertie up, her long hair fell across his face, tickling his nose and making him sneeze. "Oops! Sorry, Bertie," she apologized, flicking her hair back and scooping him into her arms.

As Mark and Sandy drove away, Gran, Gramps, and the girls saw Bertie in the back of the car, with his front paws resting against the seat, looking out of the back window and watching them as they waved goodbye.

"They seem like a very nice couple," said Gran, "and I think that Sandy is pleased to know that Bertie is going to have some responsible friends to spend time with."

It wasn't too long before Mia and the twins said their goodnights to Gran and Gramps and disappeared to their bedroom, to mull over the day's events and to plan for the following day. For once, however, Mia was not feeling chatty; there were other things on her mind, which she had yet to share with her friends.

Chapter 10

The morning after Bertie's rescue, Mia, Ellie, and Lucy woke with bright sunshine streaming through their bedroom window. They planned to stay on the beach all morning, swimming, reading, searching the rock pools and, of course, talking—their main occupation. Their special focus for the day, however, was Bertie. They couldn't wait to see him again. After lunch they read for a while in the garden, each of them checking the time every few minutes until Gramps called them from the kitchen door.

"Okay, girls, are you ready to collect Bertie?" Were they ever! They rushed up the garden, thrusting their books into their individual backpacks before slinging them over their shoulders.

"Ready as we'll ever be, Gramps," Ellie called back to him as all three friends headed for the door.

Sandy had been right; it was just a short walk. As soon as Bertie saw them walking up the garden towards the cottage, he rushed at them. With a great leap, he launched himself into Mia's arms, nearly knocking her off her feet. "*Bertie!*" shouted Sandy, who was just coming out of the cottage, "Gently does it!" Then to Mia she said, "So sorry about that. I guess he's just so pleased to see you again. I'm sure that he knew you were coming, as he has been pacing around the garden for the last fifteen minutes. Look, here's his lead and bag of goodies. I expect he will calm down when you are on your way. He's just so very excited."

Gramps, who was smiling at Bertie's antics, said, "We'll go and let you get on with your work, Sandy, and the girls will bring him home about four thirtyish, if that's okay with you?"

"That's fine. Have a good afternoon, girls, and Bertie too, of course, although I don't think that really needs saying!"

The three girls, plus Bertie, enjoyed their time together on the beach. The extending lead allowed him to race around after a ball, to explore and sniff items on the sand, and to dig for treasures. He met a few other dogs who were also on leads and so was able to exchange some "doggie talk." He even went for a paddle in the shallow waves, which surprised the girls. They had thought that after his experience the day before he might be unsure of the water and prefer to stay away from it.

Totally exhausted after an hour of energetic activities, the four friends—for of course Bertie was now a full member of the gang—found a shady spot to sit. Lucy had a bowl in her backpack, which she filled with water from her bottle for Bertie. He drank with enthusiasm and then chewed on a doggy treat before falling asleep.

"I have something to tell you both," said Mia quietly, taking advantage of a slumbering Bertie. "I was thinking about it last night in bed, and it's been in my head all afternoon." The twins looked at her with worried expressions, each of them taking one of her hands in theirs. Mia said, "Oh, don't worry, it's nothing too dreadful. But I would like to share it with you, as I know you will understand, and I don't want you to feel jealous because Bertie seems to come to me first." The twins said that they really didn't mind and that Bertie probably went to her because she had rescued him. Mia said that that might have had something to do with it, but there was more to it than that, and then she went on to tell them, "You know how Bertie seems to show me more affection?" Another nod. "Well, it's partly because I'm not a land person, like you two, but have animal—or I should say *sea creature*—origins. Because of this, Bertie feels close to me: he just relates to me as one of his kind. Don't ask me to fully explain it to you, because I can't; I don't fully understand it myself. I can only tell you what I've been told by Aunt B. She said that as a sea witch living on land, this might happen if I became close to dogs, or any other land animals, for that matter. They can apparently sense that I am different and can take to me, like Bertie has done, or even be a bit wary of me, you know, like avoid me. I can also have the same feelings about them. Like yesterday, when I was swimming towards Bertie, I could sense that he was a friend, and I wasn't afraid. I couldn't actually see anything in the water at first, but I could sense that someone or something was in trouble. It was as if he was crying out to me, and I just knew that I had to continue swimming to help him." Mia had a rather pained expression on her face as she remembered the event.

"Well, it's lucky for Bertie that you are a sea witch and could save him," gasped Lucy.

"I agree," added Ellie.

"There's more, though," said Mia. "Aunt B also explained to me that I could also start to have these feelings if a land person was in trouble, someone I knew or was close to. She said that it is a special gift that only a few sea witches possess and usually only when they are on land. Apparently, the feelings are sometimes combined with a vision, a bit like a dream.

This vision is usually about something that is about to happen—good *or* bad things." Mia stopped for breath before carrying on. "Yesterday, when Sandy and Mark came to collect Bertie, I felt a bit odd. I kept having these thoughts that they didn't quite match as a couple, and worse than that, I had a vision of Sandy tied up and in a dark place, with a red scarf or something similar stopping her from talking. It was all rather scary—the bit about Sandy, that is—so I have tried to put it out of my mind."

Each of the twins squeezed the hand that she was holding, and Lucy told their friend not to worry, because they were with her and would take care of her. "Just like we know that you would be there for us if ever we needed you. Me and Ellie are often able to read each other's minds, and we sometimes say or even do exactly what the other one is thinking or going to do. We've always been like this. It's something to do with being identical twins. All three of us are a bit odd, aren't we? Perhaps we're triplets," she laughed, and then she jokingly asked Mia the date of her birthday.

When Mia told them, Ellie and Lucy looked at each other and shouted together, "That's our birthday too!"

Lucy was the first to speak again after this revelation. "How weird is that? We were all born on the same day! Perhaps we really are triplets!"

"I can't believe it," said Mia, who was looking somewhat dumbfounded. Ellie just looked flabbergasted. Then suddenly, Bertie, who had woken up and was feeling a little left out, gave a reproachful bark that brought the girls back from their thoughts.

"You know," said Lucy, "we're just like the three musketeers—well four, really, if we include Bertie—"All for one and one for all' and all that." Mia looked puzzled and shook her head. "Never mind, I'll tell you about them later. For now, I think we had better walk Bertie home, as it's getting a little late. We can walk up to Overlook via Beaches, so Gran and Gramps can say hello to him before we take him home."

The friends linked arms and set off towards the steep steps. They climbed up to Beaches, where Bertie received a big welcome and then a not-so-enthusiastic goodbye from Gran and Gramps.

On reaching Overlook, they found the front gate open. They closed this behind them so that they could let Bertie off his lead, and they walked up to the back of the house. Finding the kitchen door open, Bertie ran inside and disappeared for a few seconds before returning to the girls, who were now sitting at the garden table. He sat down in front of them with his head tilted to one side and a somewhat puzzled look on his face.

"What's the matter, Bertie?" asked Ellie, rubbing her hand through the curly fur on the top of his head. The little dog just continued to look puzzled. Then he jumped up onto Mia's lap, giving a small whimper and nuzzling his head under her chin.

"Oh dear," sighed Mia. "I think something is wrong. Bertie's very distressed and trying to tell me something. I think I'd better go into the house to see what the problem is, as Sandy hasn't come out to us."

"Shall we come with you?" asked Ellie.

"No, I think it best if I go on my own. As the door is open, I can cast a quick spell to enable me to whiz through the rooms without anyone knowing—that is, if there happens to be anyone inside, although I have a feeling that the house is empty. Be back in a mo." And with that, Mia disappeared, only to appear a few seconds later a little out of breath. "Nobody's there," she told the twins and Bertie. "It's odd, though, as there's a cup of coffee on the kitchen table which is still warm, so Sandy must only recently have left."

"Perhaps she had to go somewhere urgently," mused Lucy. "She said that her sister was in hospital, so perhaps she had an urgent call about her."

Mia looked thoughtful. "Maybe, but I had a very odd feeling whilst in the house, as if something bad had happened." Two pairs of wide-open eyes stared at her, and Bertie rubbed up against her legs. Mia continued, "What I found interesting, though, is the very large, powerful telescope in one of the bedrooms. I had a quick look through it, and it was focused on one particular yacht in the harbour. I could see right onto the yacht and saw two people on the deck very clearly. It was two men, who were drinking out of bottles. Why do you think she was watching them?" The twins shrugged, and Mia continued, "There was also a fabulous computer system in the same room. It's like the one that my Mum and Dad use for research purposes, only much, much better. I think Sandy and Mark's work must be very important."

That Mia had managed to see so much in just the few seconds she'd been in the house did not faze the twins. In the short time that they had known Mia, they had come to expect nothing less from her.

"What'll we do now, then?" asked Ellie.

"I think we should go back home," Lucy quickly responded. "We don't know what has gone on here, or if anything has happened to Sandy, so we should go and tell Gran and Gramps that Sandy wasn't here and that we thought it best to bring Bertie back with us. We can't tell them about Mia's flying inspection of the house; we'll have to keep that to ourselves. I expect that Gran and Gramps will want to talk to Mark when he gets home from work, unless Sandy has contacted us by then. But if not, Mark may know where Sandy has gone."

Ellie and Mia agreed with Lucy, and Ellie suggested that they leave a note for Mark and Sandy asking them to phone Gran and Gramps. Lucy quickly responded to her sister's suggestion by whipping a sketch pad and pencil from her backpack. She started writing the note, letting the other two know what she was saying as her pencil quickly sped across the paper:

Hi Sandy and Mark,

We brought Bertie back home after walking and playing with him on the beach, but there is no one here, so we are taking him home with us. Please can you phone us to let us know if we should bring Bertie back later or if you will collect him?

Thank you from Lucy, Mia, and Ellie.

"That sounds fine," said Mia. "I wish my writing was as good as yours."

Lucy pulled the sheet of paper off the pad and secured it with a stone on the doorstep, where Mark could not miss it. They then debated whether or not to close the kitchen door and decided leave it open, as they had found it.

On their walk back down to Beaches, the three friends talked some more about what Mia had seen in the cottage and puzzled over Sandy having gone off without leaving any kind of message for them, as she had expected them back. They then considered that she might have called a taxi to go somewhere, maybe to catch a train, as Mark had the car, or . . . Their ideas kept coming as they made their way down the hill until they reached Beaches. But they did not come up with an answer that satisfied them.

Chapter 11

The only details that the three girls had left out when telling Gran and Gramps about their afternoon activities were Mia's quick trip through Sandy and Mark's holiday home, finding the telescope and computers upstairs, and the warm cup of coffee on the kitchen table. Gran and Gramps had been very surprised that Sandy had not been at the house and said that there was no problem with them having brought Bertie back home. In fact, they considered that this had been the right thing to do, as the girls had had no way of knowing when Sandy would return or when Mark would be home from work.

In the kitchen, Gran and Gramps were washing up following the evening meal, whilst the girls were watching television in the living room with Bertie stretched out across their laps. Bertie was a very contented dog.

"It's all rather odd," said Gramps to his wife. There was a worried expression on his face as he dried up the supper dishes. "Why didn't Sandy leave a note for the girls or telephone here, for that matter? Let's hope that

Mark makes contact with us when he gets home. He should know what's going on. I really don't mind having Bertie here but . . . well, it does seem a funny way to behave."

Gran said that she entirely agreed with him and just hoped that Sandy was okay.

After they'd finished the dishes, they joined the girls to watch Gran's favourite programme. She was not a big fan of television, preferring to read, sew, and do crosswords, but she enjoyed the quiz shows and liked to compete with Gramps to see who could get the highest number of questions right. Just as they sat down and the programme started, the telephone rang. Gramps jumped up to answer it. All eyes were on him as he picked up the receiver and Gran turned the television off.

"Hello? Oh, hello, Mark," he said nodding to the others, who were all watching and listening. "Good to hear from you. We have been a bit worried, as you can imagine, wondering if she is okay." He listened to Mark for a couple of minutes and then spoke again. "Yes, of course, please come over. See you soon, then. Bye." Putting down the receiver, he turned to the waiting group, saying, "I can't tell you much except that Sandy's fine and with her sister, something to do with her sister being discharged from hospital early. Anyway, Mark will be here in a few minutes, and we'll find out a bit more."

About ten minutes later Mark's car drew up outside Beaches. Gran opened the door for him and invited him in. She thought to herself how tired and worried he looked. He followed her into the living room and immediately apologized to them all for disturbing their day. He thanked them for being so helpful in looking after Bertie yet again. Gran assured him that none of them minded looking after Bertie at all and that their main concern was for Sandy.

"I'm not surprised," said Mark, turning to the three girls and adding, "I saw the note that you left for me—which, by the way, I would like to thank you for, as without that I wouldn't have known what was going on. I've contacted Sandy, and it seems that all is well. It appears that her sister was discharged from hospital early and needed Sandy's help with some shopping. There was no one else that she could ask, as their parents are abroad on holiday and won't be back for another couple of days. I'm hoping that Sandy will come back here when they return."

Mia couldn't help but notice Mark's face reddening as he was speaking, and she also noted that he didn't find it easy to maintain eye contact. Her witch's insight and her own intuition led her to believe that what he was saying was not exactly the truth. She felt that he wasn't actually telling them lies, but for some reason, he was unable to tell them the truth about what had gone on at the house. Gran offered to make Mark a drink and something to eat. He thanked her for the offer but refused, saying that he could only stay for a few more minutes, as he had to return to work to complete some urgent business, "I just wanted to thank you all personally for all your help and to assure you about Sandy."

"Now then," said Gramps, "what are you going to do about Bertie for the next few days? I take it that Sandy's sister won't be well enough to look after him just yet."

Mark looked surprised and then a little embarrassed, as he had forgotten all about the dog that was snoozing on Mia's lap and showing no interest in what was being discussed. He was safe, well fed, comfortable, and loved—all that a dog could wish for, as far as he was concerned. "Oh . . . yes . . . Bertie. I guess he'd better come with me," said Mark.

Then Lucy piped up. "Gran, Gramps, couldn't we keep Bertie until Sandy returns? He's really no trouble, and the three of us will look after him. I promise you he won't be a problem for you both." She glanced over at her sister and Mia, who were nodding and smiling. They were thinking, Good old Lucy.

"That's settled then," said Gramps. "That's if it's okay with my wife and, of course, you too, Mark?" Gran nodded yes, and Mark said that it was really very kind of everyone to help him out, and he could see that Bertie loved being with them and was going to be thoroughly spoiled. Bertie looked up and gave a little *woof* as if to say, It's fine with me. Then, to everyone's amusement, he jumped from Mia's lap and performed several turns, as usual not quite catching his tail, before jumping back onto the settee.

"That's good," said Mark, standing up to leave. "Bertie's sorted, so now I just have to sort myself out. I will telephone you tomorrow to let you know what's happening. It probably won't be until tomorrow evening, though, if that's okay with you all?" Receiving a chorus of "yes, that's fine" and "no probs", Mark headed for the front door.

When he was once more in his car, he brushed his hand across his brow and said to himself, "Right, Mark. Now the work really begins."

Chapter 12

After Mark had left, the three girls said their goodnights to Gran, Gramps, and Bertie, who was now resting in a large dog basket on a cosy blanket. This had been brought in from the garage where it had been stored after Becks had died.

All three girls were feeling rather tired after the day's mystifying events, and they wanted to mull it all over in the comfort of their beds without Gran and Gramps listening. Mia, in particular, was not at all happy with Mark's explanation for Sandy's absence. She pointed out to the twins that he had never mentioned how Sandy had travelled to see her sister; she certainly hadn't gone by car, as Mark had driven the car over to see them. Also, she wondered why she hadn't phoned or texted Mark earlier. The twins agreed with everything that Mia said. A frown then spread across Mia's forehead as she confided in them, "I do like Mark, and I don't get any bad personal vibes from him, but . . . when he was telling us about Sandy, I kept getting these weird pictures of her flashing through my mind's eye . . .

you know, like I told you earlier today . . . pictures of Sandy tied up in a dark place. I really don't think that she's gone to see her sister. I think that she is somewhere much, much closer."

Mia would never openly admit it, but a small part of her felt very afraid, and she was unable to control the tears that welled up in her eyes and began to roll down her cheeks.

"Oh, please don't cry," begged Lucy, jumping out of bed and putting her arm around Mia.

Ellie soon joined her, grasped both of Mia's hands, and said, "Lucy and I feel exactly the same as you do, Mia, but we know that it's worse for you because you're having these awful visions. I would be upset, and probably frightened, if it was me who was seeing them. Look, Lucy and I will get back into our own beds, and then we can carry on talking, maybe even make some plans for tomorrow until we fall asleep. Perhaps we can even think about going to look for Sandy."

Mia wiped her tears away with the back of her hand and did some deep breathing in through her nose and out through her mouth until she felt a little better. She liked Ellie's idea of looking for Sandy and thought that they should all think about the best way of doing this before they dropped off to sleep.

"I'm beginning to feel quite tired, so the land of nod sounds like a good place to be," said Mia.

Once the three friends had snuggled down under their duvets, Mia was the first to speak again. "I have this feeling that Sandy saw something happening through her telescope and that it's connected to her being missing. I can't say why I think this, as it's all mixed up in my head along with the visions. I see lots of boats—big ones like the yacht that Bertie fell off, even bigger ones, and very small ones, as well. I first got these feelings when I searched Sandy and Mark's cottage, and now they won't go away."

"Do you see Sandy on one of the boats?" Lucy asked.

"No," replied Mia, shutting her eyes, "I see her inside a dark place. with lots of nets, wooden boxes, and all sorts of other things clustered around. It could be a boat or a building. She's asleep, and she has something covering her. There's a red scarf or something like that covering her mouth, I guess to stop her shouting out." Mia let out a huge sigh before adding, "I just want to help her; she is all alone and can't help herself. She can't move because her hands and feet are tied up with rope."

Lucy and Ellie once again left the comfort of their own beds to squeeze in either side of Mia to comfort her, as well as themselves. They found what Mia was saying rather scary.

"I guess I am letting my imagination run away with me," said Mia. She could feel her heart thumping against her ribs.

"Now," said Lucy, trying to gain control, "whilst we are back in your bed, Mia, let's get down to business. What I think is that tomorrow we're definitely going to search for Sandy. I know we will all feel so much better if we do something useful. We'll have to stay here in the morning, probably on the beach with Bertie. Gran and Gramps said that they wanted to go shopping tomorrow afternoon, so I'm sure they will be happy for us to stay with Bertie. We could ask them if we could take him for a walk along by the marina and then along the creek footpath. These are the areas where there are a lot of boats moored up and also lots of others sailing in and out. What do you think?" she finished, and she took a deep breath.

Ellie still had to get used to her sister saying so much in one go. Looking at her twin, she responded to her suggestion. "That sounds like a good plan, Lucy—in fact, an excellent plan. What do you think, Mia?"

"The best," said Mia, "I'll have to go home tomorrow afternoon about six o'clock, as Aunt B will be back by then and will be picking me up, so we'll just have a few hours to look for Sandy. Having Bertie with us will be helpful. I'll talk to him so that he understands what we are doing. He loves sniffing around on the beach and in the garden, so I'm sure that he will be able to pick up Sandy's scent if we can put him in the right area."

"This all sounds so good that I can't wait to get started," said Lucy. She stifled a yawn. "Just one more thing, though. We will have to handle Gran and Gramps carefully; they mustn't suspect what we are up to. Let's get some sleep now, as we are going to need lots of energy tomorrow to find Sandy. Anyway, we will have time in the morning to talk some more about our plan, after we've persuaded Gran and Gramps to leave us out of their shopping trip."

Back in their own beds, the girls were individually going over in their minds the plans for the next day, but just a few minutes later, when Gran put her head around their door before going to bed herself, they were all fast asleep, just as Bertie was, downstairs in his basket. Gran closed the door quietly and left them, thinking to herself how peaceful they looked. If she had any idea what they had been discussing and planning, she would not have felt so calm as she closed the bedroom door and whispered, "Sweet dreams, girls."

Chapter 13

Morning came all too soon, and when the threesome didn't make an appearance for breakfast, Gran went up to see what was happening, with Bertie hot on her heels. All three were still fast asleep, but not for long! First Bertie jumped on Ellie's bed, giving her a wet kiss, and then he did the same to Lucy. Mia was spared the face licks, but he managed to wiggle his way under her duvet, where he found her feet and, of course, she soon woke up.

"Come on, girls," called Gran from the doorway. "Gramps is waiting to start his breakfast. I'll give you ten minutes to be up, washed, dressed, and sitting at the breakfast table." She then called Bertie, who popped his head from under the bottom of Mia's duvet. Smiling to herself, she went down the stairs to put the finishing touches to breakfast.

During breakfast, and as planned the night before, Ellie (who had been elected spokesperson)asked Gran and Gramps if they could go across on the ferry in the afternoon and walk Bertie along the marina front and the creek. She explained that these were places that Mia had yet to visit and that they would like to show her around. The grandparents thought that it seemed like a good idea, as they had appointments at the optician's, needed to go to the library, and had to do the week's food shopping. All things considered, they thought the girls would find this a boring expedition and so agreed to their request. Ellie, Lucy, Mia, and Bertie all said a silent *Yes!*

Rather than taking the ferry they'd decided that Gran and Gramps would drop the girls off just outside of the town centre and later in the day would pick them up at the large car park near the wharf. They considered this to be the best plan, as there were benches in that area where the girls could sit and wait if they arrived too early or if Gran and Gramps were late. It was an area that the twins knew well; they usually waited there for their grandparents if they were visiting the town together but doing different things. However, today their grandparents were going to another, larger, town a few miles away. They expected that they would be a few hours if they were to achieve everything that was on their list of things to do, so they arranged to meet at 5.30 p.m., so they could meet Mia's Aunt B back at Beaches.

When all the arrangements had been made to everyone's satisfaction, the three girls took Bertie down to the beach. They were so excited, and at the same time nervous, about their plans to search for Sandy. Mia kept having flashes of Sandy in distress and felt sure that she was in danger. Bertie was Bertie: playful, loving, adventurous, and at times naughty. Ellie and Lucy were excited about what they were going to be doing in the afternoon but kept having slight bouts of panic. To help the morning along, Lucy explained the story of *The Four Musketeers* to Mia, as she had promised the previous day. Nevertheless, the morning still seemed to drag a little. Finally, however, it was time for lunch, after which they all piled into the back seat of the car. Ellie, Lucy, and Mia each had a backpack, with supplies for Bertie, drinks for themselves, notebooks, pens, and torches. They also carried their mobiles, Aunt B having bought her niece one very similar to those that the twins used. In addition, they had money for ice creams, courtesy of Gramps.

The girls waved goodbye to Gran and Gramps as they drove away after dropping them off on the edge of the town. With Mia holding onto Bertie's lead, the foursome was soon on their way to look for Sandy. If anyone had asked them how they were feeling at that particular moment in time, they would have been given answers that included excited, worried, and a bit scared.

As soon as Gramps and Gran drove off, Mia took control. "Now, Ellie and Lucy, I will be able to look after myself, and should the need arise, I will take care of you both, as well. Providing you do exactly as I say, you will be safe. I promise you that if there is any risk of danger I will handle it. Bertie is a fast runner, so he should be all right too. Now, my fellow musketeers, we are just about ready." She looked at them fondly. "We must all have our phones ready to contact each other if we separate or if there is any possibility of danger. We can keep in touch with each other or phone the police, if that's needed. We must also have them on vibrate so that nobody can hear them." As the girls looked anxious, Mia tried to reassure them as much as she possibly could.

"Please don't worry too much, because I'm going to look after you, but I must tell you that since we have been in the town the weird feelings and pictures that I've been getting have become stronger." The twins were nodding, trying not to show how anxious they were, although this was somewhat evident by their flushed faces.

Although Mia thought that she had done a good job at reassuring Ellie and Lucy, every cell in her own body was telling her that they should turn away from this now before they got in too deep. Her sea witch's mind, however, was urging the opposite. Sandy was in trouble, and she would not be true to herself or to her heritage if she didn't do everything she could to try to help. She would have the twins and Bertie by her side, and they made a very good, strong team. Together they should be able to defeat the enemy.

Wearing her witchery like invisible armour, Mia again addressed the twins. "Phones at the ready, team," she said, pulling her own phone from her pocket and holding it out in front of her in an attempt to be light-hearted. The twins did exactly the same, and then they all set their phones to silent vibration and did a quick check to ensure the numbers that they might need were all correct.

"Right, Bertie," said Mia, giving his lead a gentle tug. "Are you ready too?" Bertie gave a gentle woof, which was his way of letting them all know that he was ready, willing, and able.

Mia again gave instructions to the team, "Twins, you know this area far better than me, so let's start looking at all the possible places involving boats where Sandy could be held. But before we start our search, I must have a talk with Bertie." Mia picked the little dog up, held him close to her, and then moved her head even closer to his, in order to whisper in his ear. The twins could just about hear what she saying. In her soft "spelling" voice, she chanted one of her magic spells:

> Little creature, small and wise,
> Please use your nose to be my eyes.
> Follow scents that will lead us on
> To the place where Sandy's gone.

When Mia had finished her chant, she faced him, nose to nose and said, "Have no fear, dear Bertie; my magic powers will keep you safe." She then put him back on the ground, saying firmly, "Right, are we ready?" The twins, despite their inner worries, chuckled as they thought to themselves that Mia really was someone to reckon with. How pleased they were that she was on their side.

Chapter 14

Ellie took the lead and suggested that they start at the marina, where there were dozens and dozens of moored yachts and as many small boats, called tenders, which were used to take the boat owners to and from their vessels. These tenders were either tied up to the backs of the yachts or were lying on the sandy shore, close to the pontoons that led to the areas where the ferries discharged their passengers or left with a fresh boatful for the various scenic trips around the bays.

It was a very busy area, only a few strides from the local shops. There were lots of holidaymakers milling around or sitting on the benches where they could eat their ice creams and other snacks whilst watching the activities in the harbour. It was also a feeding place for seabirds, which cheekily walked around the area looking for any dropped food, stopping in front of visitors, ever hopeful of a free meal. At the end of the day there were no scraps left lying on the ground.

The four friends spent about twenty minutes walking around the area. Then they decided that they had better move on, as Mia she did not feel that they were in the right place.

"I'd really love to come back here another day, when we haven't got such urgent things to do," said Mia. "It's so beautiful and interesting, and it's great seeing things as land people see them; it sort of completes the picture for me—you know, living on land but having the sea on your doorstep, with the air filled with a mixture of wonderful smells. It sort of makes me tingle all over."

The foursome continued walking around the marina area for about another twenty minutes until Mia again declared that she wasn't getting any helpful signals. So they left the marina and walked up through the main street, following several passageways down to the water, where boats were also moored. But again Mia felt nothing too unusual. Lucy suggested that they continue on up the road, as once past the shops there was a stretch without buildings where they could look out onto the bays. Again this was unsuccessful, although Mia declared the views over the water to the cliffs and the houses beyond to be magnificent. She said that she could just about see Beaches through the trees.

"We could carry on further," said Lucy, "as there are houses and hotels overlooking the water, and if we go even further up the hill, there are wonderful gardens that lead down to the estuary. What do you think, Mia?"

Mia looked thoughtful. "I'm not sure that we are in the right area. I suppose if we go higher up I could pick up some signals, but my instincts seem to be telling me that we're off-track."

"Right then," said Lucy. "I think that we should now go over to the wharf, walk around that area, and then take the road along the side of the creek. Even with the tide out, there is always plenty of water, with boats moored up. I guess it's the sort of place where someone could find a place to hide something or somebody without being seen. It's quite busy during the day, as it's quite close to the car park where we will be meeting Gran and Gramps, so there's always some people about. At night, though, I can't imagine that there would be many people around—well, not when it's dark, as most people walk there during the day to see the creek and boats and to reach the small village at the end of the road. Ellie and I have walked it many times with Gran and Gramps, as well as with Mum and Dad."

"That's right," joined in Ellie. "Last year our grandparents brought us into town for a fish-and-chip evening meal. We parked the car, and although there were quite a few other cars parked up, there weren't many people about. I guess, like us, they were there to find a place to eat in the town." Lucy and Ellie both looked at Mia expectantly, as the wharf was the last place they could think of to try. There were, of course, lots of boating areas around the coast, but they would not be able to reach them on foot even if they had the time, which they didn't.

Mia, who had been deep in thought, suddenly pulled herself together and said, "Okay, then; let's go there, but let's give Bertie a drink first and have one ourselves. I don't know about you two, but I'm very thirsty. I'd also like one of those chocolate ice cream cones," she added longingly, "but I know that we haven't got the time now." She sighed and licked her lips. "You know, the ice cream here on land tastes wonderful." The others had no argument with Mia's suggestion about having a drink. It was a hot day, and they had been walking for over an hour and a half. If the truth were known, they, too, would have liked an ice cream!

Refreshed, the team headed across the town towards the wharf. It was an interesting area of the town and, fortunately for them, it was all on level ground.

They passed a whole row of shops and workshops along one side of the narrow road, whist on the opposite side a line of terraced houses sat much higher, with steep flights of steps leading up to them. It was a busy area, with some people going about their work in the shops and others in their boat-building sheds with the fronts open for all to see in. Just about everything was related to boats. You could buy anything from a piece of rope to a yacht. There were shops selling a mixture of everyday goods as well as arts and crafts. It was an area favoured by holidaymakers, and with the warm weather, there were plenty of them about. Ellie and Lucy led Mia around the corner at the end of the road, and there before them was the car park where they were to later meet up with Gran and Gramps. As they rounded the corner, Mia suddenly stopped dead, and the others also stopped and looked at her expectantly.

"This is the place," Mia whispered. "Sandy is here! I can see her just as I've described to you. She really does need our help, and quickly!"

Ellie and Lucy kept their eyes on Mia's face. Deep furrows covered her brow, and her cheeks were bright pink, as she struggled to keep the image of Sandy alive in her mind. "I can see Sandy quite clearly, but I can't yet see where it is that she's being held." Mia stooped and picked up Bertie, holding him tightly in her arms. With her head bent down to his, she once more spoke softly to him, in the same sing-song voice that the twins had first heard when she was a tiny mermaid sitting on the shell in their glass collection bowl. They could just about hear what she was saying.

"Bertie, the time has come when you must help me. You and I must be as one. There are bad people about, so together we must work as fast as we can to find Sandy and rescue her from those who hold her captive. I see her in a dark place but cannot say exactly where it is. It could be a boat, or it could be one of these buildings around the wharf." Mia gently turned the dog around so that he was facing her. She placed her face right up to his and looked deeply into his eyes. They stayed like this for a few seconds, with neither she nor Bertie blinking. Then she placed him gently on the ground and released the lock on his lead so that he would have more freedom to explore.

Mia turned to Ellie and Lucy. "Right, now we are ready. Remember what I said to you about acting fast when I tell you. I will look after us all, but you must still be careful." Both girls nodded their understanding. They trusted Mia to do what was right.

"Are your phones ready?" asked Mia, and although they knew that they were, they each checked their own phone once again and nodded to Mia, who said in a firm voice, "Good, then let's go rescue Sandy and get the bad guys."

Although the twins were both a little anxious, to say the least, and their tummies turning somersaults, they couldn't help but giggle at their friend's last words, and Lucy said, "Oh, Mia, you are so funny, and I love your style. The bad guys just don't know what they are up against."

Chapter 15

It was still only mid-afternoon on a sunny August day, so the wharf car park was almost full. The drivers of one or two cars were looking for spaces to park, but otherwise the area was very quiet.

The three girls plus Bertie avoided walking through the car park and set off towards the area where there were many boats in dry dock. These were, on the whole, fairly smallish sailing boats and so were unlikely to have sufficient space to store a body! There were, however, a few much larger boats, but no yachts. After a walk around the larger vessels, with Bertie insisting on sniffing every one, Mia shrugged her shoulders and shook her head. They then walked towards an area where fishermen were unloading lobster and crab pots as well as other fishing equipment. Bertie sniffed some more. Mia's shoulders drooped as she shook her head yet again. Ellie then led the group to the road that ran alongside the creek where just one or two smaller boats were moored.

As they approached the road, Mia halted. Bertie and the twins did the same. Mia's keen eyesight had helped her to spot a cluster of huts almost hidden by the many shrubs and trees. There were no cars or people in sight.

"I think that we have the right place," whispered Mia. "I can see Sandy so clearly that it's making my head ache. I know that she is here somewhere." Again Mia led the group; she headed through the trees towards the first huts, pushing aside the wild plants whilst trying to avoid the nettles.

Bertie, still on the long lead, sniffed all around the first two huts and, after his thorough inspection, looked up at Mia as if to say, "Sorry, but there's nothing here."

Mia felt warm tears sting her eyes. She didn't know if she had the ability to find Sandy, and she knew that the twins were relying upon her. More importantly, Sandy was relying on her. She had only just started to develop her skills of witchery, and most of what she had learned had yet to be fully put into practice. She desperately didn't want to let anyone down, especially Sandy. So, taking a deep breath, she led the group on and the search continued.

The four went towards a single hut set further back than the others, much closer to the bank of the creek. Whilst the other huts looked more rundown, this one was well kept. They were about ten metres away from it when Bertie came to a halt with his ears standing up from his head.

"This could be it," said Mia and put a finger up to her lips to warn the twins to keep quiet. She signalled for them to stay still before giving Bertie's lead a sharp tug to encourage him to carry on towards the hut. As Bertie began frantically sniffing around the building, Mia again signalled to the twins to stay where they were.

Mia resorted to the good old-fashioned superstition of crossed fingers for good luck as she walked up to the hut with Bertie. She was thinking to herself that Aunt B would not approve of her doing this, but what the heck! There was a window at the side of the hut, but this was covered from the inside by a piece of wood which prevented her from seeing what was inside. So, with Bertie beside her, she walked around the back of the hut, where there was a second window, but this one was higher than the one at the side and had the branch of a tree partly covering it. Instructing Bertie to stay, she swung herself up by the branch so her face was level with the window. There in front of her was a small break in the glass, as if a pebble had struck it—not exactly a hole, but easy to sort out, she thought as she jumped down.

Mia walked back to the twins with Bertie and explained in a whisper what she had found. She was going to go back without Bertie. She would spell herself into the hut and have a look around. She told them that she could see all sorts of fishing stuff and lots of vague shapes under covers, but she couldn't see if Sandy was there, so she needed to check it out. Before either twin could say anything, she handed Bertie over and instructed them to now keep him on a short lead and to stay where they were. Looking at them both and giving a crooked smile, she whispered, "See you in a few minutes."

On her way back to the hut, Mia picked up a large stone. Hanging onto the branch of the tree with one hand, she stood on tiptoe and banged the stone against the cracked glass, making a hole. She stayed still, listening for a few seconds for any sound inside the hut, but she was only met by silence. She breathed in, held her breath, and then silently chanted the entry spell. When she was inside the hut, she appeared in her land form. She shivered, took a deep breath, and walked towards a large mound covered by a blue tarpaulin. As she checked what was underneath she gasped.

Mia grabbed her mobile from her jeans pocket and pressed Lucy's number. "Lucy, I'm in the hut, and I've found Sandy. Please call 999 and say that we will definitely need an ambulance and police. And ask them to hurry." She ended the call and, turning back to an unconscious Sandy, removed the red scarf that was tied around her mouth. But she was unable to undo the ropes that bound her hands and feet.

True to her word, Mia was back with the twins in exactly three minutes. She was breathless, and her face was a bright shade of pink. She took a few seconds to catch her breath and then, shaking her head as if to clear her mind, she told them what she had found in the hut, her words rushing from her mouth as her emotions tried to cope with what she had seen.

"Sandy is in there, but she is unconscious. At first I thought she wasn't there, but I looked under this old tarpaulin, and there she was. I thought she was asleep, but I couldn't wake her up, so I think that she must be drugged." Mia took another deep breath, a pained look on her face. "Both her hands and feet are tied up, and she had a gag around her mouth, a red one. I tried to undo the ropes, but they were too tight, and I hadn't got anything to cut them with, so all I could do was take the gag away so she could breathe a little better. Mia's lips trembled as she told them that they must now just wait for help to arrive. "But it's too dangerous to wait here; someone might come and find us. Let's go to the car park, where it will be safer and where we can keep an eye on this hut as well."

Ellie and Lucy were so dazed by what Mia had told them that they had difficulty speaking, so they just followed Mia as she led them away from the hut, all of them keeping an eye out for anyone suspicious. Lucy was still clutching her phone. Once they were safely tucked between a couple of boats, Lucy passed her phone to Mia, saying that when she had called 999, the police operator had asked her to keep her phone open. She suggested that maybe Mia could talk to her and explain what she had found. Mia nodded and took the phone from Lucy. She didn't say that she had broken the window or had been into the hut but got over this by saying that she had been walking Bertie and had thought she had heard someone calling for help. She said that she had climbed a tree to look through a window and had seen a woman lying on the floor who seemed to be tied up. The operator then reassured Mia that a police car was already on its way, as well as an ambulance with a paramedic on board, adding that Lucy had already given the location of the car park. She then told Mia what she had already told Lucy, to watch out for the arrival of the police and to make themselves known when they arrived, in order to direct them to the exact place where the hut was sited. Then, after a few words of reassurance, she told Mia to still keep her phone open until the police arrived. Mia said that she would.

About five minutes passed, and the friends had begun to get anxious when they spotted a man walking from behind the hut. He was dressed in jeans, a blue jumper, and a woollen hat covering his hair and pulled low down on his forehead. Green wellingtons completed his attire. He looked like a man who might be working on boats or at least have something to do with them.

As the man approached the front of the hut, he looked around him and then moved towards the door, taking what looked like a bunch of keys out of the pocket of his jeans. The twins began to panic. Mia looked startled and then took a deep breath. To the twins' amazement, the man stopped what he was doing, the bunch of keys dangling from one hand and the padlock which was still attached to the door in the other.

"Phew," said Mia, "that was close! I wasn't sure if I could remember what Aunt B had told me but looks like I got it right." She looked at the girls' stunned expressions and explained casually, "I just cast a quick spell to freeze the man in time. He will stay like that for about three minutes. I just hope the police get here before then, as when the spell wears off, he will carry on with what he was doing before he was frozen. Mia tossed her hair back, grinned, and said. "I hope you agree with me that I just performed a spectacular piece of witchery." Despite their fears, the twins also grinned, and Bertie looked decidedly happier. They were all thinking, our friend Mia certainly has good timing, and they loved her for it.

The group continued to keep an eye on the man. Suddenly a police car came driving speedily down the road towards them, and they stepped out of their hiding place so they could be seen. The car stopped as it drew level. There were two police officers in the car, and the one nearest to them had the window down. "Are you the girls who phoned in to say someone was being held in a shed or hut around here?"

"Yes, we are," said Mia, "and please, can you hurry? A man is just about to open the door." She pointed towards where the man was standing, still suspended in time.

"You girls stay where you are," said the officer as the car pulled away.

Just as the police arrived at the hut, the spell that Mia had put on the man broke. He came to, looked in puzzlement at the keys in his hand, and turned around just as the two police officers, who were now out of their car, approached him. The man panicked and started to run off.

"Not so fast," said one of the officers, who had quickly caught up with him. "We want to ask you some questions." The man looked as if he were going to try to run again, so the officers cornered him, and one of them smartly handcuffed his hands behind his back whilst his colleague took the set of keys from him, saying, "Acting on information we have received, we are going to search this building. We believe that there may be someone in the hut being held against her will." He quickly opened the back door of the police car and told the man to get inside.

With the man secured, the two officers used the keys they had taken from him, opened the door, and entered the hut. Like Mia, they found the unconscious Sandy. One officer used his radio to contact the police station, and the other set about removing the ropes that were restraining Sandy.

After another couple of minutes an ambulance arrived at the scene, and a paramedic jumped out and entered the hut, whilst the driver set about rolling a stretcher out of the back of the ambulance and following his partner. Mia, Ellie, Lucy, and Bertie watched from their position in the car park.

Chapter 16

Standing at the end of the car park where the police had told them to wait, the girls hopped from one foot to the other, whilst Bertie observed everything that was going on with great interest. As they stood watching the activities at the hut, several other people who had either been parking or collecting their cars also gathered to watch. Eventually Sandy was wheeled out, strapped onto a stretcher and covered by a blanket.

Suddenly another police car arrived, and as it passed by, the girls could see that it was Mark doing the driving, with a female police officer sitting in the passenger seat. The girls looked at each other and shrugged their shoulders, not knowing why Mark would be driving a police car. Mark jumped out of the car on reaching the ambulance and spoke to one of the paramedics. The girls could see him asking questions and nodding. Then he left the paramedics to get on with the job of taking Sandy to hospital.

Mark went into the hut and, after a few minutes, came out again and walked up towards the girls and

Bertie. "You really are the most amazing girls," he said. First, Bertie is rescued from the sea, and now you are responsible for finding Sandy."

The three friends looked embarrassed and blushed. Then Lucy spoke up. "Actually, Mark, Bertie is the hero here. He was the one who led us to that hut and sniffed and sniffed around it. Then Mia thought she heard someone call out, went and had a look through a window at the back, and, well . . ."

"That's right. If it hadn't been for Bertie, Mia wouldn't have walked around the hut and found the window," added Ellie.

Mia said nothing but nodded in agreement with what Lucy and Ellie had said. She was grateful that they had directed most of the praise to Bertie in order to protect her true identity.

Smiling, Mark bent down to Bertie and ruffled his fur. "Well done, Bertie; you are a hero." He turned back to the girls. "Now, first let me tell you that Sandy is going to be fine. Whoever kidnapped her had given her drugs to put her out, but she was already coming round when she was being put in the ambulance. Your intervention saved her from being given yet another dose of the drug. She's somewhat sore and bruised from the ropes, but otherwise she has no obvious injuries. She's been taken to hospital, where she will be thoroughly checked over before being allowed home, possibly later this evening, although she may have to stay in hospital overnight. We will just have to wait and see what the doctors think after they have examined her." Mia, Ellie and Lucy listened intently to what Mark was saying, their tummies doing flip flops.

When Mark had finished telling them about Sandy, he said, "I expect you will be wondering why and how I am here." Three heads nodded in unison, and Mark continued. "This is probably not the best time or place to fill you in on all the details, and without your grandparents being present, but for now what I can tell you is that Sandy is an undercover customs and excise officer, and I am a police officer working with her—not her husband." The girls exchanged looks; they were speechless. Mark continued, "I apologize for deceiving you and your grandparents about me and Sandy being married, but it was necessary because of the case that we are working on." Mark looked at his watch before continuing. "I'm afraid that I must go now and take the man who was arrested at the hut back to the station to be interviewed. Then I want to go and see Sandy and talk to her, if the doctors will allow me. That will fully occupy me tonight, but in the morning I intend coming to see you three and your grandparents, so I will telephone them later to arrange this."

The girls had remained quiet throughout Mark's explanations, only acknowledging what he was saying with nods, smiles, and frowns as appropriate, but when he suggested that he arrange a lift home for them, Ellie found her voice.

"Oh, that's okay, Mark. Gran and Gramps will be here shortly to pick us up as arranged. We are meant to meet them right here in the car park."

"Right, I didn't know that. I just wish I could stay and talk to them now, but I really can't wait. Please apologize to them for me. I'm sure that you are more than capable of telling them about today's events, and I will talk to them later when I phone. I may even have some more news about Sandy. Now, are you sure that you will be okay until they get here?" Three nods answered his question, and Mark finished by saying, "There are now several of my officers at the hut, and before I go I will tell them to keep an eye on you. So bye for now, and thank you for what you have done today."

Mark walked back to the hut, which was now cordoned off with yellow-and-black plastic tape. He got back into his car, and the two officers who had been first at the scene transferred the man they had arrested from their car into the back of Mark's police car. Mark got in and drove off with the officer who had arrived with him, just as a further two police cars drew into the road.

"Jiminy Cricket," said Lucy.

"Crumbs," said Ellie.

"Thank goodness that's over," said Mia. "Is life on land always as exciting as this?"

Before anyone could answer, Gran and Gramps drove into the car park. They parked their car for the girls and Bertie to get in. The girls put their seat belts on, and then Gramps started the car up again and headed for Beaches. Gran asked the trio what was going on in the car park, having seen all the police activity at the far end.

"We'll tell you all about it when we get home, if that's okay with you, Gran," replied Lucy. "It's quite an interesting story, which Gramps will enjoy more if he's not concentrating on his driving."

All three girls exchanged looks, and Mia added, "We've had a day to remember." Bertie, who was already fast asleep on Mia's lap, was making little growling noises. No doubt he was chasing bad men, Mia thought to herself, as a shiver passed through her body.

They were too exhausted to be afraid any more. All the three girls wanted was to sleep.

Chapter 17

On the journey back to Beaches, the three friends plus dog fell fast asleep. When they arrived, Gran and Gramps were reluctant to disturb them, so they unloaded their shopping from the boot of the car and put it away. Then Gran popped the meal that she had already prepared that morning into the oven. With the table laid, plates warmed, and Bertie's dinner in his dish, Gramps went out to the car to wake up the sleepyheads, who couldn't believe that they had slept so long.

"Right, young ladies," said Gramps when they were all in the house. "Before we sit down to eat, would you like to tell us about your day and why you are so tired? You must have used up a lot of energy, as Gran and I have never known you all to be so quiet—and that includes you, too, Bertie." Bertie's ears pricked up at the sound of his name, and he gave a look that let Gramps know that he agreed with him.

The girls looked at each other, and both Lucy and Mia indicated that Ellie should be the one to start.

Ellie began to tell the story of their afternoon's activities, with Lucy and Mia filling in bits and pieces to help her out. The version they told the grandparents was very close to what had actually happened. They just omitted to say anything about witches and spells. When they came to the part where Mark had appeared in a police car, Gran and Gramps were stunned. They said very little as the girls revealed the various events of the day.

Ellie finished off by telling her grandparents that Mark was going to ring them later that evening to update them on Sandy's condition. He was also going to arrange a time to see them all the next morning, to explain in more detail what it was all about.

After checking that the girls were feeling okay about everything that had happened, and having been assured by three smiling girls that they were fine, Gran and Gramps disappeared into the kitchen to discuss what they had just been told. It had all sounded like something they might see in a drama on television or read in a crime book. They just couldn't believe that the three delightful girls in the next room had tracked down a kidnapped woman with the help of a dog—such a small dog, at that—and then summoned the help needed to rescue Sandy and capture a villain.

"This has been a very interesting couple of weeks," said Gran. "I just hope that after Mark's visit tomorrow we will know exactly what has been going on. I also hope that we can then have a very quiet and uneventful few days before the girls return home."

When Gran served the evening meal, for once it was eaten in relative silence as they all sank deeply into their own thoughts. The ring of the telephone brought them all back to the present. Gran answered it. Everyone anticipated the call to be from Mark, and all four faces turned to Gran when she returned to the table a few minutes later.

"Mia," said Gran, "that was your aunt. She is being held up in heavy traffic on her way home. There's been a very bad accident involving a number of cars." Seeing Mia's anxious look, she quickly continued. "Don't worry—she was not involved in the accident, but the traffic can't move until the road has been cleared. Anyway, she has asked if you could stay here again tonight, as she doesn't know what time she will be home. I've said that we would be delighted to keep you here. Is that all right with you, Mia?" Mia nodded and smiled, as did the twins, and Gran said, "I didn't tell her about your interesting afternoon, as I felt that she had enough problems getting home without any further concerns. I thought that it would be best if we tell her in the morning. I have suggested that she join us for coffee at ten o'clock, and then we can ask Mark when he phones later if he could get here about eleven. This will allow us time to fill your aunt in about today's activities, before she hears Mark's explanations along with the rest of us. Is that okay?"

"Well done," said Gramps, and everyone else nodded.

Then a rather sad-looking Mia spoke in a quavering voice. "Thank you so much. I love it here so don't mind staying another night. After all, it will soon be the end of the holidays and we, that's me and the twins, are not going to be able to see each other until we all come to Devon again at the same time." Her lips were trembling, but she managed a smile for everyone before saying, "This is the first beach holiday that I have ever been on, and it has been the most interesting and exciting time of my life. Not only have I made some wonderful friends, but we have done some super things." There were smiles all around the table and even some hand-clapping from Gramps. To the twins, Mia sounded like the Mia that they had first met as the tiny mermaid. It seemed so long ago, but it had only been just over two weeks.

Although the television was showing one of their favourite programmes, nobody was paying it much attention. Seeing disinterest written on everyone's faces,

Gramps suggested a game of Scrabble, but nobody showed any enthusiasm. The only thing that seemed to be of interest to every one of them was his or her own wristwatch which, as they awaited Mark's call, was continually being checked and checked again, with the occasional murmur of, "It's getting late" or "Soon be nine o'clock." When the telephone finally rang, everyone jumped.

"That definitely should be Mark," said Gramps, as he got up to answer the phone. He left the room, leaving the door open so the others could listen in to his end of the conversation.

After about five minutes or so, Gramps was back in the room, having finished the call by saying, "Okay, Mark, see you tomorrow about elevenish." Everyone looked at him expectantly as he came back into the room. "Well, as you may already have gathered," he said, "Sandy is recovering well. The drugs the kidnapper injected her with have mostly worn off, but she is still a bit groggy. She has no serious injuries, just a few bruises, which is bad enough but not life-threatening." Everyone let out huge sighs of relief, and Gramps continued, "They have contacted Sandy's real husband, who is returning early from a business trip abroad. He should be here by tomorrow afternoon to be with her. Apart from that good news, there is nothing else I can tell you, as Mark would like to tell us the full story tomorrow. He said that he would explain as much as he could then. Oh, and just one more thing. He hopes to collect Sandy from hospital in the morning and bring her here with him, as she wants to thank you three girls personally for what you have done for her."

Everyone started talking at the same time; the hubbub woke up Bertie. He sat up, got out of his basket, put his head to one side, gave one of his funny barks, and jumped up onto Mia's lap.

"Yes, you too, Bertie," said Mia, giving him a cuddle. "You played a huge part in our finding Sandy. You should get all the praise."

Everyone said that they agreed with this, but although the twins agreed outwardly, they knew that without Mia and her spells Sandy might still be lying on the cold, dirty floor of the hut or something even worse could have happened to her. This thought sent a huge shivers down their spines.

"I just wish", said Lucy, "that we could know what it has all been about now and not have to hang on until tomorrow, but I guess there is nothing to do but just wait." There were nods all round. Then Gran said that she would give Mia's aunt another call to find out how she was getting on and to confirm the times for the next morning.

Aunt B had just reached home and been about to phone them. She agreed to be at Beaches around ten the next day.

Everyone was very tired after such an emotionally draining day, and so the three girls decided to go to their bedroom now that all the telephone calls had been made.

As it was going to be the last sleepover at Beaches, Gran and Gramps had agreed that Bertie could sleep in the girls' room, and Gramps carried the dog basket up the stairs.

All four occupants of the bedroom were soon tucked up in their beds and were asleep almost immediately, exhaustion having got the better of them. All talking would have to wait until the next day. The four would-be musketeers had outwitted and fought the enemy, won the battle, and were now *zzzzz*ing their way through the night . . .

Chapter 18

After a sound night's sleep, the twins and Mia were awakened by the sun streaming through the large bedroom window; they were immediately excited about what they would be hearing later from Mark. They were all looking forward to Aunt B's arrival as well, although Ellie and Lucy were still a little wary of her and couldn't help but wonder how she would react when she heard about their previous day's escapades.

When breakfast was over, everyone moved into the garden, where Gran had laid out cups and glasses on the large old garden table, ready for their guests.

At 10 a.m. precisely Mia's aunt rang the front doorbell.

After all the hellos, kisses, hugs, and handshaking had been completed, everyone sat around the table. Gran poured coffees and cold drinks as requested. Then the events of the past two days were relayed by Ellie, Lucy, and Mia, before Gran and Gramps told her what they had arranged with Mark.

"Well," said Aunt B, with her head on one side and her green eyes sparkling, "it sounds as if I've missed out on a great deal of activity whilst I've been away." Then, turning to the twins' grandparents, she apologized to them for having left them to pick up all the pieces.

"Not at all," said Gran. "Gramps and I didn't know anything about it until it was all over, so we haven't had to do anything other than agree to Mark coming here this morning. We had your mobile number, but we didn't think that it was worth bothering you. The main thing is that Sandy is safe and the three girls came to no harm." She smiled at Aunt B before continuing, "I hope that you agree with me and my husband that all three girls have behaved very responsibly. Bertie too, of course. What a wonderful bloodhound he has turned out to be."

Everyone laughed, and Aunt B gave her niece a sidelong look that caused her to shuffle on her seat.

The doorbell sounded for the second time that morning, making everyone jump a little. Gramps quickly got up to answer it. He returned a few seconds later with both Mark and a rather tired-looking Sandy, who had been determined to be at the meeting. She hugged the girls in turn, thanking each of them, before Gran introduced her and Mark to Mia's aunt, whom they had not previously met. As Sandy shook hands with Aunt B, she felt a sharp tingling sensation travelling up her arm, which she put down to her recent trauma. After giving her hand a little shake, she picked Bertie up into her arms, rubbed her cheek against the top of his head, and told him what a wonderful dog he was. When Sandy had finished and everyone was settled, Mark began his explanation.

First of all, Mark told the group that he was Detective Inspector Mark Baker and that he was usually based in one of the larger seaports along the Devon coastline, where he worked together with Customs and Excise in trying to prevent some of the illegal importation of drugs. Mark paused and looked expectantly at his audience, fully expecting a barrage of questions. When none came, and he saw that everyone was just waiting to hear the next part of the story, he continued.

"As you can imagine, the sea provides a great opportunity for villains who want to bring drugs and other illegal items into this country. Boats of any kind provide ideal vehicles for this activity. Local police in these coastal areas where boats are continuously coming in and going out of the marinas and harbours work very closely with Customs and Excise officers, who have a huge job on their hands. Would-be smugglers can also make a lot of money bringing in illegal immigrants.

Sadly, these people are often transported in very poor conditions." Mark looked around at all the faces hanging on his every word.

"This is how I know Sandy. We are currently working together on a major case. Sandy is trained to look out for unusual behaviour in people who come in and go out of the harbour on what appear to be privately owned yachts with innocent holidaymakers aboard them." He stopped for a while to take a sip of his drink. The room was silent, so he thought it best to quickly continue. He looked at Sandy and smiled broadly before saying, "This young woman is one of the best in her field of work and has been responsible for uncovering several illegal drug-importation scams, leading to the arrest and imprisonment of the would-be importers. She is amazing, and I think that you should hear from her about what she has been up to—that is, if you feel up to it, Sandy?"

Sandy, who had looked very pale when she'd arrived, blushed at Mark's flattering words. Saying that she was fine, she readily took over from him. "I think that Mark has already told you that we are not married as we led you to believe the first time we met, when we collected Bertie. We had, you see, rented the holiday cottage as a base from where we could work. I have a powerful camera-linked telescope, computer system, and other equipment which I use in my work, and that cottage gives an excellent view of boats coming in and out of the estuary. I could follow their movements and get descriptions of people on them and so on. We decided that we would say that we were man and wife, as Mark needed to be at the cottage with me quite a lot when we were observing various boats that were giving us cause for concern. That way it saved any need for further explanations, for as you can imagine, we didn't want anyone to know what we were actually doing."

Sandy paused for breath, and then she turned to Mia, Ellie, and Lucy, asking them, "Do you remember that day that you rescued Bertie from the sea?" The girls nodded. "Well, the woman I was with on the yacht is also with Customs and Excise, and she and her work partner were also keeping watch on the marina from the yacht they were on. The day Bertie fell overboard, her partner had gone off to a meeting with Mark, and she and I were studying videos and other information that she and her partner had been collecting over the previous weeks."

Sandy blushed once more, saying, "I am sorry that we had to tell you a few fibs, but at that stage of our operation everything was extremely secret." As she smiled, her whole face lit up. "But Bertie really is my sister's dog, my sister really is in hospital, and I really do have a husband—just not Mark." Everyone laughed with her, which relieved some of the tension.

Mark took over again, speaking for both himself and Sandy, as he could see that she was looking tired.

"So now that you know who we really are and what we do for a living, have you any questions?" he asked. Nobody had any; they just wanted to hear more, so he met their silent wishes.

"When Sandy was on the yacht with her colleague, someone saw her and recognized her." Saying this caused Mark to frown, but he went on, "A couple of years ago, Sandy was involved in a case where she had to give evidence in court, and in fact, she was the key witness. To cut a long story short, the two main defendants were found guilty and were sent to prison for several years. One other man, who played a minor part in the offence, also went to prison but was recently released. At the time he was sentenced he was very, very angry, with Sandy in particular, at being found guilty because of her evidence. He swore that he hadn't been involved. Sandy's evidence however, showed that he was lying. At this stage, we believe that he may have been involved in the kidnapping of Sandy and that maybe he had spotted her on the yacht in the harbour. I'm afraid we can't tell you much more than this, as we do not want to compromise the case against him, especially as there may also be others involved. We want to make sure that we catch them all. Kidnapping is an extremely serious offence." Mark stopped talking for a couple of minutes to take a breather and have a sip of water, allowing the group to talk amongst themselves.

Everyone settled down as Mark continued, "The man who was caught at the hut where Sandy was being held does not seem to have been involved in the kidnapping itself. However, the hut does belong to him. He claims that he was being paid just to keep an eye on Sandy, we think by the man I just mentioned. The man at the hut also claims that he hadn't wanted to get involved but had a lot of pressure put on him by the other man. Nevertheless, he knows that he is in big trouble and has told us all he knows about the kidnapping, hoping that it will help his case when he goes to court. What we have yet to find out from him is how much he and the kidnapper were involved in illegal drug importation. I can't tell you exactly what he has told us so far, but let's just say that he has been very helpful, and just about any minute now," he said, looking at his watch, "Customs and Excise will be boarding a yacht not many miles from here that we believe may be carrying a large cargo of drugs." Everyone gasped before Mark concluded that he was afraid that he and Sandy must leave. "I need to find out what's happening at the yacht, but not before I take Sandy home to the cottage. Her husband should be there any minute now, and we don't want him sitting outside and worrying, do we?" he asked everyone.

"My goodness," said Gramps, being the first to speak. "What a tale you have told, and to think these three girls have played a major part in it all it . . . it's unbelievable."

"Yes, it is," said Gran, and Aunt B nodded her agreement, her eyes focusing on her niece.

Mark and Sandy stood up to go, and Sandy, looking at the three girls, said, "If you hadn't found me, goodness knows what might have happened. So I want to thank you all again so very, very much, and Bertie too, of course." Hearing his name mentioned, Bertie did one of his attempts at barking and chased his tail. Everyone squealed with delight at his antics. For such a small dog he really did have a talent for taking the tension out of a situation. Finally they'd all said their goodbyes, and Mark took Sandy and Bertie home.

After Mark and Sandy had left, Aunt B said that she and Mia must go too. They had several things to do in the gallery, as well as starting the preparation for Mia's parents' and brother's arrival at the weekend. However, she promised to come over with Mia to the beach the next morning so that Mia could spend some time with her two friends. Each of the three girls looked a little glum at the prospect of their holiday reaching its end.

After everyone had left, Beaches felt surprisingly empty and quiet, even though there was lots of talk going on about what Mark and Sandy had told them, as well as speculation as to what was going to happen to the villains, as Mark had described the bad guys. Gramps said that he expected the illegal drug importers would have to spend many years in prison, as would the person or persons who had kidnapped Sandy.

Chapter 19

The following morning, Aunt B and Mia arrived as planned. She had driven over today rather than take the ferry. Mia was clutching a large brown paper-covered parcel, which she handed to Gran and Gramps who had decided to spend a quiet morning sitting in beach chairs watching the world go by. When they opened the package they gasped on discovering one of Aunt B's paintings, the one she had started of the view across the estuary on the first morning with them all on the beach.

Gran and Gramps were overwhelmed. They hugged Mia and her aunt. Mia told them that the painting was to thank them for all their kindness, sleepovers, and lovely food during the holiday. Aunt B added that she thought it would go well with the picture they already had. Gran and Gramps wholeheartedly agreed with her and said that they couldn't wait to hang it.

They all had a relaxed morning talking, paddling, and just generally doing not very much at all. The three girls talked together about what they had learned from Mark and Sandy and Aunt B; Gran and Gramps did the same. Just as Aunt B and Mia were preparing to leave, they saw a man and a woman with a small white dog, held on a lead, walking towards them.

"Hi," said Sandy and hugged them all in turn. "This is my husband, David." After all the greetings that also included wet kisses from Bertie, Sandy handed each of the girls an envelope.

"David bought these vouchers for you at the airport on his way home yesterday. I'd been able to speak to him on his mobile and told him that I wanted to give you all a present for saving me. We both thought that you would like to buy something for yourselves rather than receive something chosen by us, and we thought that vouchers would be a good idea."

When the girls opened the envelopes and looked inside, all three of them jumped in excitement, and they gave Sandy a huge team hug. Then they looked at David and gave him one too, causing him to go bright pink. "Wow!" he exclaimed. "I never expected that."

Sandy spent a few minutes telling everyone that yesterday's raid on the yacht had been very successful, with a huge quantity of drugs having been found, and four people arrested who were currently being held in police custody for questioning. "You can probably read all about it in tomorrow's papers or maybe hear about it on the news tonight. So, well done, Mia, Ellie, and

Lucy—without you it might never have happened. Oh, and you too, Bertie, my little hero." Bertie sat up and accepted the praise. He was really getting used to all this attention.

Goodbyes were finally said. Sandy and David left to go back to their holiday cottage, and Aunt B and Mia went back to Aunt B's home in the town. Everyone was a little sad at the goodbyes, and each one spent the rest of the day mulling over in his or her mind all of the events of the last few days. Ellie and Lucy's thoughts went right back to when they had found the little sea witch in their glass bowl.

Chapter 20

It was the last evening of their holiday in Devon, and the twins had packed up all their belongings. They were experiencing exactly the same problem with zipping up their case as they'd had when they were packing to come away on their holiday, but this time they knew how to solve the problem. Closing the case was also helped by the washed and ironed clothes that Gran had done for them and which laid flat in the case; the crumpled items that they had packed for themselves were underneath.

Their parents arrived as planned. They were going to spend just one night at Beaches and would make the journey home with their daughters the next morning. Their arrival took away some of the sadness that the twins were feeling about leaving Devon and their grandparents, but mainly they felt sad about the separation from their special friend Mia. They were going to keep in touch with her through Aunt B, who had promised that she would pass messages back and forth for the twins and Mia. Without Aunt B's help there was no way that Ellie and Lucy could have had direct contact with Mia once she had returned to Shellamac. They were going to miss her so much. At Aunt B's home, Mia was experiencing the same thoughts and sadness at leaving Ellie and Lucy.

The twins' parents heard all about their daughters' friendship with Mia and were also treated to the tale of Bertie's rescue, the kidnapping and all that followed. They just sat there open-mouthed.

The next morning, they said their goodbyes to Gran and Gramps, and the family set off for home. As the car was pulling away, Gramps took his wife's hand in his, turned to her, and said, "It's been such a busy three weeks, with so many interesting things happening, and I don't know about you, my dear, but I am absolutely exhausted. I just want to sit in my old armchair, put my feet up, and watch a really boring programme on TV."

"Me too," agreed Gran.

Chapter 21

Back home in Somerset, the twins spent their time preparing for their return to school. There were dentists to be visited, items of uniform and shoes to be bought, and school bags to be located and filled.

Lucy, in particular, was looking forward to the new school term. During her time in Devon she had managed to put behind her all the bullying she had endured during the previous year at school. She knew that she would never let anyone bully her again. Her experiences with Ellie and Mia had helped her to control her fears, and she felt that she could see off any bullies should the need arise. After all, she had helped in Sandy's rescue from kidnappers, and by doing so had contributed to the arrest of drug smugglers. Not bad for a twelve-year-old girl who had, only a few weeks ago, been afraid of her own shadow.

The few days leading up to their return to school passed slowly, but then the day arrived. They looked good in their school uniforms, their white blouses showing up the golden tans that they had gained on holiday. Their hair was pulled back into the usual bunches, but now Lucy sported a fringe, like Mia's. Their mum and dad drove them to school on their way to work and dropped them outside the school gates, wishing them a good day before driving off to their jobs at the local hospital.

Once inside the school building, Ellie and Lucy were soon caught up in the excitement of seeing friends, finding their lockers, and joining the scramble for seats in the classroom where they would spend a great deal of the school year. They managed to find places next to each other on the front row, and the class settled down as Miss Bellamy, their new form and English teacher, entered the room. After taking the register, Miss Bellamy announced that, as a gentle introduction to the new school year, she would like everyone to write an essay. Picking up a piece of chalk, she wrote the title up on the board. It read "What I found exciting about my summer holiday".

"Now class," she continued, "please try and use those brains that have been having a rest all summer. Make your essay exciting, something that we would all like to hear, something that would make us laugh or cry, for that matter, but definitely something original. Right. I now have to go to the Head's office for a few minutes, and when I return, I expect to see you all hard at it."

Ellie and Lucy looked at each other, and Lucy whispered to her sister, "Even if we could tell, no one would believe us."

To this Ellie replied, also in a whisper, "You take the dog rescue, with a few changes, and I'll write about the shell that . . ." Lucy looked aghast at her sister. "Just joking," said Ellie, laughing. "I'll think of something not quite so interesting." They chuckled to themselves, shrugged their shoulders, and got on with the task in hand.

When Mrs Bellamy entered the room about ten minutes later, all heads were down and she could hear the scrape of pens on paper. "Class," she called out, "can you put your pens down for a minute?" Everyone did as they were asked, although there was some annoyance at having had their literary flow interrupted. "I would like to introduce a new girl who will be joining us."

Ellie and Lucy both raised their heads, and then their mouths dropped open, as they saw the familiar figure of Mia standing by Miss Bellamy's side. She was dressed in a brand-new school uniform, and her blonde hair was tied back in a thick plait. Her sparkling eyes the colour of the Devon sea seemed to light up the whole room.

"This young lady is Mia," said the teacher. "Please ensure that she is helped to settle in. Now, Mia, I suggest that you sit between Ellie and Lucy. Ellie, you move to the empty desk next to you to make a space for Mia, and Lucy, will you please tell Mia what the essay is about and ensure that she has paper and a pen?"

Ellie, Lucy, and Mia had but one thought: School life is going to be very interesting this year!

When the twins had an opportunity to talk to Mia later in the day, they learned that her parents, whilst on holiday, had discussed moving to live on land. At the conference they had attended in Switzerland, they had met a number of doctors, two of whom were the twins' parents. They had told them about positions that were available at a new medical research centre where they lived in Somerset. As their son, Gi, was about to go to university, Mia's parents had already given serious thought to living on land themselves for a few years, and as Mia had enjoyed her time with her Aunt B and had made good friends with Ellie and Lucy, they felt that she would not have too much trouble adjusting to life as a land girl over a longer period. Applications for jobs were made, a house found just a few streets away from where Ellie and Lucy lived, and a place gained at the same school they attended. Mia and her family were now prepared for their new life.

Chapter 22

As she entered the long corridor where the pupils' lockers were situated, Mia's sharp eyes spotted Lucy at the far end talking to a girl slightly tall than her, with light brown hair. She thought that it was a girl called Donna, who was in the same class as herself and the twins, a girl who didn't seem to mix much with the other pupils. Mia's witch's instincts immediately told her that something was wrong. In the bat of an eye, she had joined the two girls. Seeing the worried look on Lucy's face, she asked her if she was okay. Lucy's frown vanished when she saw Mia, and a smile lit up her face. Lucy replied that she was fine and that she and Donna were just having a chat about homework. Gently taking hold of Lucy's arm, Mia asked if she could show her to the sports equipment storeroom, as she had been sent by the sports teacher to collect a hockey stick.

"Sure. No problem. It's just further along on the same corridor as the classroom where Donna and I were heading."

The three girls walked together in silence. Donna went into the classroom, whilst Lucy took Mia to the room that she was looking for.

When they were on their own, Mia asked Lucy what the problem was between her and Donna. Lucy looked uncomfortable, as she didn't like breaking confidences, but she knew that she could trust Mia, and she was just a bit unsure about what Donna had asked her to do.

"Mia, it's really nothing much. It's just that Donna wants some help with her homework assignment, the one we have to hand in on Friday." Seeing the worried look in Mia's eyes, she quickly continued, "She said that she hasn't started it yet and that she will get into trouble if she doesn't get it in on time, as she's been late with the last two assignments. She was just about to tell me why when you arrived."

Mia looked concerned and, putting a hand on Lucy's arm, asked her if Donna had been bullying her.

"Oh no!" said Lucy, a pained expression on her face. "Donna's not like that. She knows what an awful time I had last year with bullies; she would never hurt me, I feel sure. We actually get on very well. Anyway, I said that tonight I would jot down some of the research information that I have used and a few other things that might help her. I'll give the notes to her tomorrow, and hopefully that will help her get started. She is actually a very clever girl and usually does well with her homework, so I don't know what's going on with her."

Mia looked thoughtful before saying, "Well, if you're sure you want to help her, then that's up to you, but if Donna is usually a hard worker, perhaps there is something causing her a problem, and we need to find out what that is, if we really want to help her."

Lucy nodded. "Perhaps she will tell me tomorrow," she said hopefully.

As Mia picked up a hockey stick, she said, "Right. Now, if you're sure you're all right, I'd better get back to the sports field; otherwise, I'll be getting into trouble myself." Mia grinned, wrinkled her nose, and disappeared, stick and all. Lucy stood looking at the empty space left by Mia and chuckled to herself. She was thinking, good old Mia, if she could avoid using up any energy, she would. She was right. Mia was back on the sports field before Lucy had even closed the door behind her, and the only muscle she had used was her nose.

Lucy headed for the classroom. A sprained ankle had meant her missing hockey. Instead she had to spend the afternoon reading in one of the classrooms. Donna was also in the room, having cried off sports because of a headache, and she was sitting with her head resting on her arms. There were one or two other girls in the room with them, as well as a teaching assistant keeping watch, so there was no opportunity for Lucy and Donna to talk that afternoon.

Donna tried not to think about what she had just done. She hadn't wanted to ask Lucy to help her, and she certainly hadn't wanted to involve Mia, someone who had only arrived at the school three weeks ago and who scared her just a little, although she wouldn't have been able to say why if asked. There was a part of her that didn't like herself very much for asking Lucy to help her, and she certainly didn't want anyone else to know about it, but if she failed to hand in this latest assignment she would be in big trouble, and she wanted to avoid that. She had enough problems in her life as it was.

Chapter 23

The following morning, Lucy clutched two sheets of A4 paper on which was written the information that she had promised Donna. She just had time to hand them over to Donna before class started, Donna having arrived in class with only minutes to spare. Donna took the papers and mouthed a silent "thank you" as Miss Bellamy arrived.

The young and attractive sandy-haired teacher sat at her table in front of the class and told them to take out their personally selected books. These were books which they should have been reading as part of their ongoing homework over the past few days. She wanted them to spend the lesson making notes about the story, ready to present a brief outline to the class the next day. For Lucy, Ellie, and Mia this wasn't a problem, as they had already completed their books. Also, Mia had a remarkable memory and if asked would be able to quote the whole book word for word. Some of the other girls, who were not such keen readers, sighed and exchanged looks, with eyebrows raised. Miss Bellamy chose to ignore all of these silent protests. Everyone started the work—that is, except Donna, who sat with a distressed look on her face, thinking, Now what am I going to do? I've not even started my book!

Normally Mia wouldn't have had second thoughts about making someone squirm for asking Lucy to do work for them, but as she looked across at Donna, she could sense that something was making her unhappy, and she immediately felt sorry for her.

After morning lessons, Donna went into the recreation room, ate her sandwiches on her own as quickly as possible, and walked over to where Ellie and Mia were engaged in a game of chess. Lucy, unable to cope with the intricacies of the game, sat reading a book. She was so absorbed that she didn't immediately see Donna standing in front of her, not until she spoke.

"Hi, Lucy," Donna said quietly, her voice quivering. "Sorry to bother you, but can we talk?"

"As long as you don't want me to do any more work for you," replied Lucy, for once not looking particularly friendly.

"No, it's not anything like that," said Donna as her eyes filled with tears. Lucy immediately felt bad about her sharp response and invited Donna to sit next to her. Donna sat on a spare chair; her face was flushed and tears were rolling down her cheeks.

"First, I want to say sorry. I don't want to make excuses but . . . well . . . you are so clever and . . ." She wiped her eyes. "I was gonna skip lunch to study for Friday's homework . . ." She held up a book so Lucy could see it. "I'm not trying to avoid the work . . . it's just that I don't seem to have time to do it." Donna lowered her eyes, clearly embarrassed. "I'd like to tell you why I'm in such a mess and can't get my homework done—that is, if you would like to know and if you are even interested, for that matter. I don't mind telling your sister and Mia, too, as I know that you are all friends."

"Please don't upset yourself. I know you wouldn't have asked me if you hadn't been desperate," said Lucy.

"Never," said a rather subdued Donna.

As Ellie and Mia were near to Lucy and Donna, they had seen the tears and witnessed Lucy taking hold of Donna's hands. Other pupils in the room were too involved with their own conversations and activities with friends to be bothered with anything that was happening around them, but Ellie and Mia shuffled their chairs, making a circle with Lucy and Donna.

Lucy spoke for Ellie and Mia as well as herself when she assured Donna that if they knew what was going on then, they might be able to help in some way. Donna nodded, and Lucy looked at her watch. Seeing that there was just fifteen minutes left of the lunch break, she suggested that Donna should use the time to fill them in.

Donna started to talk, grateful to at last be able to share what had being weighing heavily on her shoulders for several weeks. She told them that her mother had been ill and was still in hospital after an operation. Donna had been looking after her younger sister and brother, as well as the house, for the past four weeks. A friend of her mother's, Ginny, came each evening after she had sorted out her own family. She slept at the house and left early the next morning to go to work.

"What about your dad?" asked Ellie.

"Dad works on an oil rig off the Scottish coast, and Mum didn't want to worry him, but Ginny made contact with him last night, and he will be home on Friday when Mum comes out of hospital." She gave a sigh of relief. "I've been doing all the work in the house, getting meals, and seeing the kids off to school—and a lot more things." Her shoulders slumped as she continued, "I've been helping Mum with all the chores since she got ill and have felt too tired to think of homework. In class sometimes I nearly fall asleep." She looked up at the three pairs of eyes watching and hanging onto her every word. "I'm not complaining, but I can't wait for Mum to come home, and Dad, too. I really wanted to get the house sorted, and Ginny said she would try to help tonight, as we don't want Mum to find a mess and feel that she has to start cleaning before she has fully recovered. So I guess it's payback time for me," she finished, giving a rather weak smile.

"What do you mean?" asked Ellie, her face showing the same concern as was reflected on Lucy and Mia's faces. The three had been shocked by what Donna had told them.

"It's just that I'm unlikely to be able to clean the house, feed the kids, and do the ironing, as well as all the other things that have been piling up. My homework will never get done, even with the help Lucy has given me, so it serves me right for trying to cheat." Just at that moment the bell called them to lessons, and there was no more time that day to talk to Donna, as she left quickly to get home for her brother and sister.

On their own way home, Lucy said she felt a little guilty about Donna and her situation; she felt that she had been a little hard on her. Ellie got cross with her, saying that she shouldn't feel guilty, as she had done nothing wrong and had even given her notes to work from.

"I know that, but I can't help feeling sorry for her," replied Lucy irritably. The rest of the journey was spent in silence as each of the three friends mulled over what Donna had told them and tried to think of ways to help her.

Chapter 24

That evening as Mia was working on her homework, every couple of minutes Donna popped into her thoughts. Little did she know that Lucy and Ellie were having the same problem. After struggling to complete half of her work, she suddenly had what she thought was a brilliant idea. It just popped into her head. "I must phone Ellie and Lucy," she said out loud. But before she could pick up her mobile, a call came through from Lucy.

"Hi, Lucy! I was just about to call you and Ellie, as I've had a brilliant idea about helping Donna."

"Same here," said Lucy. "You go first."

"Well, I was thinking, if we missed swimming tomorrow, we could go home with Donna and help her sort out her messy house. It shouldn't take long with four of us. Donna will then have enough time to do her homework ready to hand in on Friday."

"I don't believe it! That's just what we thought," Lucy squealed, "although we thought that you wouldn't want to miss swimming night, knowing how much you love it."

Before Lucy could say any more, Mia told her that on this occasion she wouldn't mind, if it would help Donna, and it was agreed that they would suggest it to Donna at morning break the next day.

At Donna's home, the younger children were in bed, and Donna was about to make a brave attempt to tidy up the kitchen before Ginny arrived, but there was such a mess that she didn't know where to start. In the end, she just sat and cried until she had no more tears. She sobbed, "Oh, Mum, I really miss you and promise when you're home I will do everything that I can to help you. I will never moan about doing chores ever, ever again!"

For Donna, morning came too soon, and she was tempted to turn off the alarm and go back to sleep. Instead she flung the duvet back, woke the younger children, and padded downstairs to sort out breakfast. There was just one thought in her head—only one more day before Mum and Dad were home.

On their way to school that morning, the twins and Mia decided that, providing Donna agreed to their plan, they would go home with her after school the following day. Mia suggested that Lucy and Ellie should each take one of the younger children and get them started on their bedrooms whilst Mia would clean the kitchen and Donna the other downstairs rooms.

"That's a lot for you to do, Mia," said Ellie, "as I expect that includes the washing—" She stopped, a cheeky smile coming over her face. "Oh, I get it! You will have a little extra help."

"Right," replied Mia. "I can't even keep my own room tidy. Mum won't let me call upon my witch's powers to help out. It's a house rule—but she didn't say anything about sorting out messes in other people's homes using the odd nose wiggle or suitable spell."

Lucy wasn't able to catch Donna until the first break period arrived, and then she quietly asked Donna if she could have a word with her. Donna looked puzzled and a little nervous, as she was still feeling guilty about the previous day, but she nodded her agreement. When they met up, Lucy explained the plan to Donna, who looked at her in puzzlement.

"You would really do that for me, after what I did to you?" she asked, her cheeks turning bright pink.

"Look Donna, we understand why you did what you did, and it's all forgotten. If you don't want our help, we won't be offended, but—"

Donna quickly interrupted to assure Lucy that she would love some help.

"Fine," said Lucy. "We will come home with you tomorrow after school. Three extra pairs of hands should make a difference, don't you think?"

"Oh yes," replied a smiling Donna.

Chapter 25

Mia and the twins accompanied Donna to her home. When the bus dropped them off, they had to wait a few minutes for Donna's brother, Timothy, and sister, Lara, to arrive on their school bus. The younger children were surprised when Donna introduced her classmates to them and told them that they were going to help tidy up the house. But they were soon chatting to them about things that had happened at school that day and complaining how hungry they were.

Donna's home was a large red-brick cottage set amongst similar dwellings. Donna opened the front door and led them all into a very large kitchen. Immediately the others could see what Donna's problem was. It was a shambles. Mia and the twins' hearts dropped into their boots as they surveyed the mess. They knew that upstairs things probably wouldn't be any better.

Whilst the others were taking off their coats, Donna quickly put the kettle on and found some clean mugs and plastic cups, which she placed on the table, at the same time collecting up dirty ones. She found a loaf of bread, butter, sandwich fillings, and juice in the fridge, explaining as she buttered the bread that the children were always hungry when they came home, so she made their tea early. She carried the plates of food and two cold drinks into the family room, where her brother and sister were watching television.

Returning to the kitchen, Donna found that Lucy had made a pot of tea for them all. Donna produced a tin of biscuits, and the four of them sat at the kitchen table to discuss the cleaning arrangements. Donna raised no objections to the plan, and when they finished their snack, Mia was left to her own devices in the kitchen.

Mia surveyed the enormous task before her and then sat in one of the two comfy chairs that were placed either side of the fireplace. "Right, where to start?" she said, thinking out loud. "Yes, a spell should cover all of this", and her spell voice rang out:

This kitchen needs to be clean and tidy
For Donna's mum, who's home on Friday.
Dishes washed for another day,
Floors swept and mopped, toys put away.
Dirty clothes in the washing machine
Dried and folded when they're clean.

When she'd finished the chant, Mia sat back in the chair, clicked her fingers, and watched with a smile on her face as the kitchen changed into a spotlessly clean room where everything was in its right place. Clean, dry, pressed clothes were stacked on top of the washing and drying machines.

"Phew," said Mia, "that was hard work. Now I think I deserve a rest," and she picked a newspaper from the now-very-tidy stack by the side of the chair. As she opened the paper, a quiver spread from her hand, along her arm, and over her whole body. It was something she referred to as her witch's intuition, a signal that all was not right in her immediate world. She gently allowed her right hand to hover above all the items of news, turning pages as she did so. She did not notice any deeper tingling of her fingers until she reached page 7, headed Local Business News. When her hand was over a picture of a group of people standing outside of a newly opened coffee shop, the tingling feeling was so strong that her hand felt as if it were on fire. Mia quickly pulled her hand away and studied the picture, but there was nothing unusual, just two young women and one youngish man in black T-shirts and trousers. There was a large motif on the front of the shirts. They were standing in front of the shop window, bright smiles on their faces. Then she saw it, the reflection in a second window, the face of a man who looked older than the others in the picture. Mia hesitantly placed a finger on the man's image; she had to quickly pull it away as she felt a pain shoot along her finger and arm. At that precise moment the kitchen door opened, and in walked Donna. Mia quickly put the paper down.

"Wow, this kitchen looks fantastic! How on earth did you clean up the mess so quickly?" said Donna. Then she spotted the neat stacks of freshly laundered clothes and, with a gasp, added, "You've washed, dried, and ironed the clothes, as well. Oh, Mia, you are a very fast worker! I can't believe that you've have done all of this. You must have a magic wand or something," she finished with a laugh. Mia's face had turned very pink as she sought to give Donna an explanation without giving her secret away.

"I get it from my Mum," she blurted. "Her job demands a lot of her time, so she has learned to do things at high speed and has passed her techniques on to me." This, Mia thought, was actually the truth, although not quite in the way Donna thought.

"Well, you must show me sometime," laughed Donna, a bewildered expression still on her face as her eyes darted over the shining kitchen surfaces. "Now, what did I come in here for? Oh, I remember, a fresh can of air spray." She fetched one from a cupboard, continuously glancing around the kitchen and thinking, Mum is going to be knocked out when she sees this!

When Donna returned to her chores, Mia had another look at the picture in the local paper. She did not recognize any of the people being photographed nor the man whose face was reflected in the window. What she did know was that the feelings she had just experienced were exactly the same as those she'd had when she and the twins were on holiday and searching for Sandy. She just knew that the man in the picture was connected to that dreadful crime. But she and the twins had thought everyone concerned with the kidnapping had been arrested and that they were in custody awaiting trial. She folded the paper and placed it on the table, to remind her to ask Donna if she could borrow it. She glanced at her watch, and as it was still very early, not quite half past four, she thought that the rest of the cleaning party might need a helping hand— or, preferably, a slight twitch of her eyebrows or nose.

Mia found the twins struggling to sort out Tim and Susie's bedrooms, so she first sent Susie to help Donna downstairs and then, with a short spell, transformed the girl's bedroom into a wonderfully tidy child's palace. Ellie chuckled as items of clothing flew around the room, settling themselves into the wardrobe, drawers, and linen basket as appropriate. Most amazing was how the bed suddenly looked as if it should be in a posh bedding store. Mia turned to Ellie, saying, "Well, that's one bedroom sorted."

"Thank goodness for that," said Ellie, jumping for joy.

After shooing Tim out of his room, Mia repeated the bedroom clean-up, rescuing Lucy from a mountain of cars, trains, and comics. Lucy clapped her hands as the floor was suddenly cleared. Even a raggedy teddy bear seemed to be smiling as he sat on top of the now-immaculate bed.

"Well done, Mia," said a happy Lucy. "If you hadn't come to the rescue, I think I would have gone off the idea of ever having children." With lips pouting, she heaved a sigh of relief.

On her way back to the kitchen, Mia stopped at each room and completed whatever still needed doing. The bathroom and shower rooms now gleamed.

Donna's room received minimal attention, as it was already clean and tidy. "Unlike my room," murmured Mia as she closed the door behind her. Finally Mia opened the door to the main bedroom where Donna's parents slept. Like Donna's room, it didn't need much help. The only finishing touch Mia made was to leave a bunch of fresh flowers in a vase on the dressing table. "Perfect," she said, closing the door behind her, "but just one more thing to do." And Mia cast yet another spell, to ensure that the house remained clean and tidy until Donna's mother was strong enough to cope with household chores.

When everyone was back in the kitchen, it was only five o'clock.

"I can't believe that we have cleaned the whole house," said Donna, looking at Mia and the twins. "I can't think what I would have done without you. Now I just have to get some supper ready and make sure that Timothy and Lara get to bed early and get a good night's sleep, ready for Mum's return tomorrow morning." Donna wiped her eyes with the back of her hand before continuing, "Now I will have lots of time to do my homework. I've already told Miss Bellamy that I will be late in tomorrow and the reason why. She said that it would be fine, provided I go in for the afternoon lessons and hand my assignment in." She then hugged Mia and the twins.

Mia felt a little embarrassed by Donna's profuse gratitude, knowing how little effort she personally had put into the cleaning. To cover her embarrassment, she picked up the newspaper that she had left on the table and asked Donna if she could take it with her, explaining that there was an article that she wanted to read about a new café in the town.

Donna said that she could take the paper, adding that she had been in town with her mum on the day the café had opened. They had seen a photographer taking pictures of the staff. The new owner had refused to have his picture taken and gone back inside the café. Then, when the local paper had arrived that week, her Mum had laughed, as the owner's image showed up through the window. Donna finished by saying, "Mum heard from someone that he was moving into the large cottage at the top of our road, the one with the wooden gates. We've never seen him, but since he's lived up the road he has had lots of visitors. Mum said that he was probably having café supplies delivered there, as he has a large brick garage that would be useful for storage. Of course, we don't know; we're just guessing, really. He might have lots of friends."

Chapter 26

After saying their goodbyes, the three friends stood in the lane outside of the now spic-and-span cottage. Lucy turned to Mia and grinned. "Mia, you're a miracle worker," she told her.

"Seconded," added Ellie "but *ple-e-ease* never, never, never offer us up to clean those children's bedrooms ever, ever, again. It's the very worst chore that I have ever had to do!"

"Ditto," Lucy said with a laugh.

"Okay. Got the message," Mia said with a grin, "but how about my room? I really could use some help with it. Mum has threatened to bag all my clothes up and bin them unless I tidy it soon." She pulled her mouth down, trying for a sad look but only succeeding in looking mischievous with her sea-green eyes sparkling. "Okay, just kidding! Actually, I've got a plan: I'm going to call my brother, Gi, to spell it tidy for me, as Mum won't let me do it that way for myself." The twins looked at Mia in disbelief; then all three laughed until their sides ached. When they had gained control of themselves,

Mia spoke again, "You think I'm joking, don't you? But I'm not. I really can't stand it in my room. It's so bad I can't find my best shoes, the ones with the kitten heels that Aunt B bought for me." When they had finally stopped laughing, Mia's voice became soft and song-like. It was her witch's voice, and the twins immediately knew that Mia was about to do something that she could only do if she stepped into her witch's persona.

"I've got another favour to ask," she whispered. "I want to go and have a look at the cottage at the top of the lane and, if possible, go inside for a good look around." Seeing the looks of astonishment, mixed with fear, on the twins' faces, she quickly told them what she had in mind.

"I'll go up to the front door and ring the bell or knock to see if anyone is there, and if no one answers, I will need to see if there is an open window so that I can get in. If you walk halfway up the lane with me, I will do the rest. Just keep one of your phones ready to let me know if you see anybody coming. I'll have mine on vibrate." She looked deeply into her friends' eyes, and having assured herself that they understood what they must do, she finished by saying that she couldn't explain why she was doing this but would tell all later. Ellie and Lucy closed their mouths and nodded. They trusted Mia.

They hadn't walked far before Mia told them to wait and said she would go the rest of the way on her own.

"Okay," said Mia, "here we go." One minute she was standing with them and then the next she was gone. The twins looked at each other and shrugged their acceptance. They had been there before, in Devon; nevertheless, they clutched each other's hands for comfort.

The twins hardly had time to find a place amongst the hedging where they couldn't be seen when Mia was back with them. Slightly breathless and with her face flushed, Mia stood in front of them.

"Well, that was a bit of a waste of time," she said and she sighed. "I managed to get into the house, as the bathroom window had been left open just a crack. The only unusual thing about the house was that there was no furniture, other than an unmade bed in one of the bedrooms and one of those metal rails with some man-size clothes on it, but nothing to show that anything dodgy is going on there." Then, frowning, she said that she hadn't been able to see inside the garage as it had no windows, and the front door and the door between the garage and the house were locked with heavy bolts and padlocks. "Mind you, I did get a very strange feeling when I placed my hand on the handle of the garage door," she finished, a look of satisfaction on her face.

The threesome walked back up the road to catch the bus home. They sat on the back seat, where they could talk without anyone hearing. Mia took the newspaper out of her bag and opened it at the page showing the café. Pointing to the reflection of the man in the shop window, she told the twins what had happened in Donna's kitchen, how she believed the man was connected to Sandy's kidnapping, and how the house she had just visited belonged to him.

"I got such a strong feeling when I touched his photo that I am certain this man was involved."

"What shall we do?" asked Lucy as memories of Sandy's kidnapping flashed through her mind. There was no answer from the other two, just slight shrugs of shoulders. All three sat quietly, frowning whilst trying to think of a solution to the problem.

"I've got it!" said Mia, making the other two jump. Both turned to hear what Mia had to say, expectant looks on their faces.

"Okay, let's hear it then," said Ellie.

"Well, you know you are going to be staying at my house tomorrow night," said Mia. Ellie and Lucy nodded. "We'll ask my mum if we can go into town on Saturday morning. I'm sure that she'll let us, as she trusts me when I am with you two. We can go to the café, order some drinks, and just sit there for as long as we can. Hopefully the owner will be there or at least come in whilst we are there."

"Good idea, and if we have our phones with us, we can take a few photos of each other and try catch him in one of them," added Lucy enthusiastically.

"Great thinking, you two," joined in Ellie. "We should be able to get some good shots of him between us."

That decided, they spent the last few minutes of the journey discussing what they would wear. "If only I could find my blue shoes," moaned Mia.

For Donna, Friday went according to plan. She arrived for the afternoon class carrying a folder, which she handed to Miss Bellamy with a huge smile. Between lessons, she managed a few words for Mia, Ellie, and Lucy. "Mum's home, tired but fine. She couldn't believe how clean and tidy the house looked, so I told her that I'd had some help from a few school friends. She says to thank you, especially for the flowers in her bedroom." Ellie and Lucy pointed to Mia, who looked rather embarrassed. Donna continued, "I also got my homework done—and without using your notes, Lucy. So sorry you went to all that trouble for nothing."

"No probs. I'm just glad it all worked out for you in the end," said Lucy.

Before the lesson began, Donna just had time to tell her three new friends that they were "the best".

Chapter 27

It was Saturday morning, and for once the Mia was awake early and ready for the day ahead. Crawling out from underneath her duvet, which was laden with tried on and rejected clothes from the night before, she went over to the large blow-up bed that the twins were sharing and bounced on the end of it, shouting, "Wakey, wakey, sleepyheads! Time to get up!"

Groans came from the shapes under the duvets, and two tousled heads appeared. "Thought we might as well get the show on the road," said Mia.

"But you're usually the last one up," responded Ellie, yawning.

"I know I am, but I also know that today is going to be both exciting and satisfying. I feel it in my witch's bones that we're going to catch the villain."

The three washed, dressed, and got ready for what the day ahead held for them. They had dressed for a warmish late-summer's day in jeans and favourite T-shirts, topped off with a green hoodie for Mia, a pink jumper for Lucy, and Ellie's favourite blue cotton sweatshirt. All three wore colour-coordinated DMs that they had bought with the vouchers Sandy had given them at the end of their holiday.

Breakfast over, Mia enlisted the twins' help to tidy her room, a chore her mother had insisted upon before they went out. When they had finished, Mia declared their joint effort "not half bad", claiming that it would last until Christmas.

"You're so lazy," shouted Ellie.

"Too right," agreed Lucy.

"I know, but you love me," said Mia with a giggle.

Chapter 28

For eleven o'clock on a Saturday morning, the centre of town was rather quiet as the trio walked towards the café. Peeping in through the glass door, they saw that there were only a couple of customers and no sign of their "target", so they decided to do a bit of window shopping and try again later. After about half an hour they returned to the café, but there was still no sign of the man, just the two female assistants.

"Shall we go in for a drink anyway?" suggested Lucy. "I wouldn't mind a hot chocolate." She met with no argument from Mia or Ellie. They chose a booth halfway down the room, where between them, they could keep an eye on the whole room. The hot chocolate drinks that they had ordered were placed in front of them.

"I feel a fat bum coming on," said Ellie as she gazed at the masterpiece in front of her, but Lucy and Mia were far too busy spooning off their marshmallows and whipped cream to reply. Ellie, who was facing the door, had picked up her phone to take a picture of Lucy and Mia. She looked up when she saw the door of the café opening, and recognizing the man, she angled her phone so that she could catch him in the frame. *Click*, and there he was, captured on-screen, with Lucy and Mia's heads in front of him.

"He's just come in," whispered Ellie, holding her phone so the other two could see.

"Well done," said Mia. "Now let's see if we can get some more, but be careful. Don't let him see us snapping him."

The man stood talking to the two members of staff at the bar, and so there was plenty of opportunity now for Mia and Lucy to snap him behind Ellie.

"I think that should do," said Mia. "Now we need to get home and send these to Sandy." They finished their drinks and left.

The previous evening, as they lay in their beds, the three friends had agreed that, if they managed to get any pictures of the man, they would send Sandy an email saying that they were out and about in town, had stopped for a milkshake and taken some pictures which they thought she would like to see. Lucy, who had offered to do the typing, added other bits and pieces which she thought would make the letter more natural. Before signing off, she added, "Don't know how the man got in the pictures; he just kept bobbing up as we were clicking. Apparently, he is the owner of the café and actually lives at the top of the road where one of our school friends lives." She gave the name of the road and described how nice the cottage looked with its large wooden gates. She then signed off with their three names. Ellie and Mia approved the email, and Lucy sent it off.

"Let's hope that if the man in the café is one of the kidnappers, Sandy recognizes him," said Ellie.

"I'm one hundred percent sure that she will," said Mia, her eyes steely and determined.

Chapter 29

Sandy was in her office in Plymouth, putting the finishing touches to a report she'd had to prepare regarding her work in Devon. She was just about to pack up and go home when her computer announced an email. When she saw who it was from, her heart gave a leap of pleasure and anticipation. She always loved the emails her three young friends sent her. She read the email before opening the attachments. A smile spread across her face as she saw the pictures of the twins and Mia—and then the smile disappeared as she saw the man the girls had captured in their photos. She placed her fingertips on the man's image, and the equivalent of an electric shock ran along her arm. She jerked away and immediately picked up her phone and asked Mark, who was working in the next office, if he would come to her room, as she had something to show him. Hearing the urgency in Sandy's voice, Mark stopped what he was doing and joined her.

"Come and see this," said Sandy, pointing at the computer screen. "He's changed his hairstyle and grown a moustache, but I would know him anywhere! His face is in my memory bank."

Mark also recognized the man who they believed to be responsible for Sandy's kidnapping. Initially he was lost for words. Then, pulling himself together, he managed to speak. "I don't know how three young girls managed to get pictures of the man half of our police force are looking for, or what made them give us his address if he was just a man in a café they were visiting, but frankly, I don't care—as long as they are safe and we have a chance of arresting the man who kidnapped you!" He thought for a minute before deciding on the next step he and Sandy would need to take. "Right," he said, "I'm going to lift the man's images off the girls' photographs and send them to my colleagues in Somerset, together with the information about the café and where he might live. I'll not say where it came from, as we don't want Mia or the twins involved in any way. This is a nasty man we are dealing with, and the children's safety is of the utmost importance. Hopefully the police can pick him up quickly and hold him for questioning."

Mark checked that Sandy was okay, as she had just had a shock and was very pale. He suggested that she go home and told her he would let her know how things developed.

As her husband was away on business, Sandy arrived home to an empty house. Normally she loved his company in the evening, but tonight she thought that it was just as well that he was away, as she had a lot to think about. She changed from her work clothes into casual clothes and furry slippers, made herself a cup of coffee, and relaxed on a large leather settee. While her coffee cooled, she lay back and shut her eyes, pulling up memories of her kidnapping in Devon and her subsequent recue in which Mia, Ellie, Lucy, and Bertie had played a major part. She could hardly bear to think about what might have happened to her had it not been for them finding her.

When Sandy had first met the three girls, she had felt an immediate closeness, to Mia in particular. She couldn't say why, but it was there. When she had been close to her, she had felt something like pins and needles passing through her body. When she had lain bound and gagged on the dirty floor in the fisherman's shed, although drugged, she had felt Mia's presence. Throughout her life, she had occasionally experienced other physical experiences like the one she had had when she'd seen the girls' pictures of the man. And when she'd touched the face of the man on the computer screen, an unpleasant tingle had run along her arm. Previously when something like this had happened she had put it down as a nervous twitch. But after it had happened several times, with each one coinciding with her helping to locate sea vessels that were involved in drug trafficking, she had begun to wonder if there was more to it. But what?

Sandy sat up to drink her coffee, at the same time remembering when she was a very small child sitting on her grandmother's knee and being told how many, many thousands of years ago their family had been sea witches. Her grandmother had been a wonderful storyteller and always made the stories exciting as she told of sea witches rescuing drowning sailors. She never tired of these stories, at the end of which her grandmother would say, "Now, Sandy, you must never tell anyone what I have told you. Do you understand?" Sandy had always nodded her head, indicating that she did, and her grandmother would finish by saying, "When you meet one, Sandy, you will know." And each of them would put a hand to their mouth and say, "Shh."

Sandy smiled to herself as she remembered her grandmother and her tales. Then the smile disappeared, and she silently asked herself if it could be true what her grandmother had told her. Was she descended from sea witches, and was Mia a sea witch?

"Don't be so silly," she said out loud to herself. "There's no such thing as a sea witch; it was just a story made up by my grandmother to entertain me." *Still*, she thought, that tingling I sometimes get is very odd!

Later that evening, after Sandy had cooked and eaten her evening meal and was relaxing in front of the television, her mobile buzzed. It was Mark.

"Hi there, Sandy. Do you want the good news or the bad news first?" he asked.

"Might as well get the bad news over and done with," replied Sandy with a deep intake of breath.

"Well," said Mark, pausing for effect, "there is no bad news, but the good news is that the police have picked up the man from the photograph the girls sent you, and they have him safely at the police station waiting to be interviewed. As he has asked for his solicitor to be present at the interview, and as she isn't available until tomorrow morning, he'll be in the cells overnight. He's worried enough to wait for his solicitor, so I have a feeling that we'll get a result." Sandy could almost see the smile on Mark's face as he added, "And there's more. A team of officers are now searching his house and garage, thanks again to the details the girls gave you. He wouldn't give his address at first, but when he was told that we already had it, he gave up his keys."

It was obvious from the tone of Mark's voice that he was happy with how the Somerset police were handling things, and he went on to say that he would be going to Somerset in the morning to sit in on the interview and would let Sandy know the result the first chance he had.

When Sandy turned her phone off, she felt like a tonne weight had been lifted off her shoulders. "Thank you, Mia, Ellie, and Lucy," she said. "You've done it again."

The following morning, Sandy sent off a long email to the three friends, talking about everything but the man in the photo, as it was important to keep the girls' names out of the investigation, just as they had done in Devon. But in her heart Sandy knew that the girls would be aware that the information they had sent to her had been acted upon. Local papers would then confirm it all for them in a few days; it would be a main headline, she felt sure.

Chapter 30

The Monday after Mia, Ellie, and Lucy had sent their email to Sandy, school seemed all too quiet and normal. During lunch break they were talking about joining the drama group, who were to put on a pantomime at the end of term to raise money for charity. Mia, who was looking very thoughtful, said that she hoped Mr King, the drama teacher, would select the story of *Sleeping Beauty*.

"Why that one?" asked Ellie, pulling a long face. "I find it rather boring."

"Me too," added Lucy, puckering her lips.

Mia's eyes twinkled, and a smile formed at the corners of her mouth before she answered. "Well, I thought if it is to be that pantomime, I would audition for the part of Sleeping Beauty, and then, if I was selected, I could just lie on a comfy bed and snooze for most of the play."

Ellie and Lucy laughed and playfully slapped at Mia's arms. "Oh, Mia, you really are a very lazy witch," Lucy whispered, seeing Donna heading towards them.

"Hi, you three. Mia, do you remember that café that you were interested in?" Mia nodded, and Donna continued, "Well, the new owner was arrested at the weekend, and there were police cars going up and down my road most of Sunday. Dad went up to try and check what was going on and could see that the police had the garage open and were taking away lots of boxes and all sorts of other things."

Mia, Lucy, and Ellie all tried to play it cool as they responded to Donna's news, but their stomachs were churning with excitement.

It wasn't until the three friends were alone on the bus home that they could talk about Donna's brilliant news.

When the local paper dropped on the doormat on the Wednesday morning before school, Mia scooped it up. On the front page, in bold print, was the headline local man arrested and charged with kidnapping!

"Yes!" she said under her breath as she set off to join the twins at the bus stop.

Lightning Source UK Ltd.
Milton Keynes UK
UKOW05f1646121113

220934UK00001B/18/P